THE BROKEN TRAIL

A HARRIET HARPER THRILLER

DOMINIKA BEST

THE BROKEN TRAIL
HARRIET HARPER THRILLER SERIES - BOOK 3

Copyright © 2020 by Dominika Best

ISBN: 978-1-949674-10-1

www.dominikabest.com
First Edition

For Dave
without you, none of this would be possible

ALSO BY DOMINIKA BEST

PROLOGUE
OCTOBER 19, 2018

Addison James did not want to be out in the middle of Hollywood tonight. She flexed her fingers remembering the tune she was working on. It was a tricky chord progression she wanted to get right by next week's lesson with her mentor, a jazz legend by the name of Foster McGuire.

Sophie, her best friend since fifth grade, had called begging for support earlier. So instead of playing her guitar, Addy was waiting on a small patch of grass across from the Scientology Celebrity Center right off of Franklin Avenue. Supposedly, that's where Sophie's producer told her to meet him for the most fabulous party of the year. Or so Sophie had said.

Sophie had that hopeful tone in her voice when she told Addy about how she'd met some big hotshot producer at her acting audition earlier in the day and he'd invited her to a party. Addy knew her friend thought this invitation might be the ticket to getting a part in the newest superhero movie, but Addy highly doubted that. The casting couch was a real thing, and

Sophie had already encountered enough lecherous creeps in this town to know better. But Sophie was her best friend and when she'd begged, Addy was afraid Sophie would just go alone if she didn't agree to be her wing woman. So, Addy put on a sparkly dress, applied her makeup to look just like a model going out to a nightclub, and put her light-brown curls into a loose bun. She borrowed without asking her mom's highest black heels and real diamond stud earrings and headed out.

Sophie might be a dead ringer for Megan Fox, but she was also street smart. She wanted Addy there for back-up, just in case. Addy doubted she could be of much help, yet here she was at the side of a road, waiting for a chartered bus to shuttle them into the Hollywood Hills for the supposed party of the year.

The bus was a nice gesture, but that didn't make Addy feel much better. How would they leave? When she'd brought this up, Sophie brushed it off, saying they could walk out and call a car service before mentioning again how excited she was to finally be invited to one of these exclusive parties. The way Sophie said that finally convinced Addy to come along.

Sophie slipped her hand into Addy's and squeezed. "Thanks for coming with me, sister," she whispered into her ear.

Addy smiled and squeezed back. "Do you know those girls?" Addy whispered, nodding to three girls walking toward their corner, definitely dressed up for a party.

They saw Addy and Sophie and waved. The tall red-haired girl in the middle smiled.

"Are you two going to Jimmy's party?" she asked.

"I don't know a Jimmy." Sophie shook her head. "The producer that invited me is Thomas Brown.

"Don't know him, but this party is supposed to be going off," the blonde next to the leggy redhead said. She looked like a taller version of Pamela Anderson. Their gorgeous black friend, dressed in a suit and looking uncomfortable, didn't say a word. She wanted to be there as much as Addy did.

A small white bus drove up to the little group and opened its door. A young guy was driving.

"You ladies ready to party?" he asked.

"Hells yeah, baby," the blonde-haired girl said.

The quiet woman rolled her eyes at her friend.

"Is this for Jimmy's party?" the red-haired girl asked.

Addy noticed a slight tremble in her voice. Jimmy must have promised her something spectacular, she thought.

"Don't know the hosts, but if you're on this corner, I'm supposed to be picking you up," he said with a wink.

Addy didn't like the sound of that. She wanted to be home. Sophie squeezed Addy's hand.

"You ready?" she asked.

"As ready as I'll ever be," Addy said and followed her best friend into the van.

The white van drove up a winding, seemingly one-way road into the Hollywood Hills. Addy had never been to this part of the Hills and understood why the hosts had chartered a van for their guests.

For one thing, the neighbors would complain about noise, congestion, and parked cars, and she was sure the cops would shut the party down. Rich people didn't like to have strangers at ragers in their neighborhoods.

After about fifteen minutes of driving, the white van finally stopped.

"Be careful up there," the driver said as he opened the door for them.

When Addy turned back, she saw him frown. Her stomach knotted. Why was the driver frowning?

Addy watched the three girls make their way up the steep drive in their heels. Sophie started up right behind them. Addy took a few steps and frowned. Her fancy stilettos had been a bad idea. They were made for sitting and looking hot and not teetering up a gravel driveway.

"See you gals up there," the redhead called out to them and the three girls disappeared over the crest of the hill.

Sophie looked back at Addy and noticed her struggling to walk. She skipped back and put her arm around her. "Thank you so much for coming with me," she said.

"You said that before." Addy laughed. "It's gonna be fine," Addy said even though she didn't entirely feel like it would be. She heard the distant techno music pounding and her stomach swirled with nerves. Addy had only turned seventeen last month, and she'd already been to her share of parties.

This one felt different, though. Maybe all the information coming out through the #metoo movement about girls assaulted and abused by well-known Hollywood men could be putting her on edge.

"All right, let's do this," Addy said.

The friends hiked up the drive and the party unfolded in front of them the moment they made it to the top.

"Holy shit," Addy said under her breath.

The mansion was a replica of a small castle made of rough-hewn stone like the ones she'd seen pictures of in Europe. The grounds were immaculately manicured with flowers and hedges. Beautiful, young people, drinks in hand, mingled under twinkle lights. Addy could see couples kissing in secret rock grottos against water fountains. The aroma of marijuana smoke mixed with the scent of roses. And it was only eleven o'clock.

"What kind of party is this again?" Addy asked as they headed toward the front door.

A drunk girl bumped into them and laughed. "Oh my god!" She laughed. "Your skin is flawless. How old are you girls?" she asked, peering into their faces.

"You're drunk," Addy said.

"What's it to you?" Sophie asked and pushed past her.

"You toddlers know this is a swingers party, right?" she called after them. Addy stopped and turned around.

"Wait, what?" Addy asked. "What exactly is a swingers party?" She knew she sounded naïve and stupid, but she didn't care. Swingers were married couples who swapped partners, right? None of these people looked too old.

"What is she talking about?" Addy asked.

"She's drunk, honey," Sophie said under her breath.

Addy knew Sophie well enough to tell when she was changing the subject.

"You brought me to a sex party? Eww." Addy shuddered.

Sophie stopped walking and pulled Addy to the side.

"What the hell, Sophie? You knew about this and you still made me come?"

"Well obviously, I couldn't go alone," Sophie hissed. "And no one made you come. I really want this part, Addy. We don't have to do anything."

"Obviously," Addy said. "Eww again. These guys are way too old. Let's just find this producer of yours and get it over with as far as your presence being here is concerned."

"Thank you, Addy," Sophie gushed. I owe you big time."

As they turned toward the front door, Addy looked up and saw a toned, acrobatic woman twisting gracefully between two straps of silk hanging from a tree. The completely nude aerialist had an intricate butterfly tattoo that seemed to flutter its wings as she whirled. Addy had never seen a woman move like that before, and she couldn't turn away from the spectacle.

Addy's eyes grew wide as the woman spread her legs out into a split showing her female bits to anyone in the crowd below her. Something sparkled and Addy saw that right above her genitalia were crystals shaped into a star, glittering and casting their reflection as she moved.

"Holy shit," she whispered to Sophie. "Are you seeing this?"

"Oh my God, she's doing that naked," Sophie said, covering her eyes with her hands.

Addy scanned the crowd. "All these guys are like in their thirties and forties," she said.

"You said that already," Sophie commented. She was also scanning the crowd.

"Do you see your producer anywhere?" Addy asked. The longer they were here, the more Addy wanted to be home.

The men definitely skewed toward receding hairlines and belly paunches. The women on their arms, however, were young and gorgeous.

Wasn't that always the case in Hollywood, Addy thought. As expected, the women looked impeccable, their bodies slim and toned, their skin, hair and makeup perfection, while the men were slobbish, wearing shorts and sneakers with unkempt hair.

"I don't see him." Sophie shook her head. "Let's go inside."

Addy tore her eyes away from the naked aerialist and followed her friend inside the mansion. Even though the castle looked huge on the outside, on the inside it was cramped with people and dark.

"I think I see him," Sophie said over her shoulder and disappeared into the crowd.

Addy tried to follow her friend, but the crowd closed in around her. As she pushed through in Sophie's direction, she overheard three girls and a guy discussing who would go first. In what, Addy didn't want to know.

She finally pushed through into a larger room, but Sophie was long gone. Great, Addy thought. Now what was she going to do?

She wandered to the bar and smiled at the bartender wearing a white shirt and a black bowtie. If nothing else, she could at least get a drink. "Is this an open bar?" Addy asked.

"Indeed, it is," he said. "What'll you have?"

He didn't ask her age or to see an ID. She supposed that was a good thing.

"Can I have a glass of white wine?" Addy wasn't really a big drinker. Occasionally when she and Sophie did manage to get alcohol, it was white wine Sophie pilfered from her mother. Addy could handle a glass, and she certainly didn't want to get drunk here. The bartender handed her a wine glass of yellow liquid.

"Enjoy," he said with a smile.

Addy turned away from him and took her first sip. The cold liquid rolled down her throat and her body responded by warming right up. She turned to the dance floor and watched as couples grooved to the music in front of her. At least for the most part everybody was wearing clothes here.

"You look lost," a man's voice came from her right.

She turned to see a good-looking guy, probably in his mid-thirties, holding a bottle of beer.

"I lost my friend," Addy called out, trying to make herself heard over the music.

"I lost my friends too," he said. "My name's Peter."

"Addy," she said.

"We can find your friend together," he said.

Addy looked him over again. He didn't look dangerous, but then again no one got into Ted Bundy's car because he looked dangerous.

"What about your friends?" Addy asked.

"Forget them." He laughed. "Who needs 'em?"

"Really?"

"Actually." He leaned closer to her and loudly whispered. "I think they want to be alone."

"Oh, I see." Addy nodded.

"Are you an actor?" Peter asked as they pushed away from the bar.

"Musician," she replied. "My friend Sophie is an incredible actor. A producer invited her to this party. I'm just the sidekick."

"You don't look like just a sidekick to me," Peter said. "You should think about doing acting yourself. You have the most beautiful eyes."

Addy flushed at his compliment and then was immediately embarrassed. She wasn't a stupid little girl to fall for a line like that, right?

"Sure, right." She laughed. "I gotta find a bathroom first. Be back." She pushed away from him. As she made her way through the crowd, she could see Peter following her in the mirrored wall.

Great, she'd have to find a way to lose him somehow. Her stomach knotted again and she wanted to puke up the white wine she'd just finished. Where the hell was Sophie? Why did she come with her? She could be home chatting with Nick, her crush. Or learning that new song her mentor had assigned her. Instead, she was at a weird party in a stranger's house trying to ditch some thirty-year-old skeeve.

She walked faster and pushed through the crowd, nearly knocking a drink out of someone's hand. Where the hell had Sophie gone to anyway?

1

DAY 1 – MONDAY, NOVEMBER 5, 2018

L APD Detective Harriet 'Harri' Harper sat at the Nickel Diner flipping through her latest cold case while she waited on Detective Jackie Render for lunch. As a detective in the Cold Case Homicide Special Section (CCHSS) of the Robbery-Homicide division of the Los Angeles Police Department, Harri took on cases that had gone cold, using new techniques like DNA matching to bring justice to long-forgotten victims. Her current cases included a woman strangled in her apartment in 2004 and a drive-by murder in Hollywood in 2000. Neither of them would be solved by running DNA.

The cold case haunting her the most though, she hadn't solved. Not yet. She had found her decades-missing older sister's body some months back up in an Oregon national forest. Now, she needed to find and bring to justice who pulled the trigger.

"Sorry, I'm late Harri," Detective Jackie Render said as she plopped down in the seat next to hers. "Working lunch?"

Harri smiled at her friend. As usual, Jackie was

perfectly manicured with her hair swept back in a groomed ponytail and bright red nails with red lipstick to match. Harri had once asked how Jackie could look so put together with two small girls at home while working Special Assault Section (SAS) of the Robbery-Homicide division. SAS dealt mainly with Sexual Assault, the most disturbing cases in the department in Harri's estimation.

"Something like that," Harri said.

"If you don't mind me saying so, you look like shit," Jackie said.

Harri smoothed down the brown strands of hair escaping out of her own ponytail.

"But you've had a rough few months." Jackie shrugged.

"I finally found her," Harri said. She hadn't spoken to Jackie since she'd gotten back from Oregon several months ago. She'd kept a low profile after the shitstorm she'd dealt with at the LAPD. Special Agent Nick McNarin, who'd been in charge of the missing boys case up in Oregon, had called everyone he knew in LA to get rid of her after her investigation into her sister's disappearance collided with his dormant investigation of a number of boys who'd gone missing in the same area. Harri thought he should be appreciative that she'd practically solved both cases, but McNarin didn't see it that way.

And he ended up knowing a lot of people. Specifically, Richard Byrne, the detective who most wanted her out of her job.

"It was a beautiful funeral," Jackie said.

Harri nodded. The Oregon coroner released her sister's body three weeks after she and Jake Tepesky arrived back in Los Angeles. Both she and Jake, a former FBI profiler, had been investigating the trafficking ring since then, trying to put names to the men who'd killed her sister and those boys.

"Any leads?" Jackie asked.

"Nothing definite yet." Harri shook her head. "That's part of the reason I wanted to talk to you. You've worked cybercrimes, right?"

"I have." Jackie nodded as she looked at the menu. "They found the guy who murdered those kids up there, right?"

"Yes," Harri said. "But not the sickos who put together the entire operation. The FBI got involved."

"Ready to order?"

Harri looked up into the cheerful face of the waitress and gave her order. After Jackie asked for more time, the waitress left them with a nod and a smile.

"I heard about that special agent calling every bigwig he could get hold of," Jackie said.

"I'm sure everyone down at the PAB heard about that," Harri said bitterly.

"If they hadn't, then I'm sure Richard made it his business to make sure everyone who needed to hear it, did."

Detective Richard Byrne and Harri had a long history of animosity after an encounter years ago. He was the one who'd managed to keep her out of Homicide for the last several years. In short, he was a prick.

"What do you need to know?" Jackie asked.

"Most of these crime syndicates that traffic children have gone online?"

"Like everything else." Jackie nodded. "Vice is a business, so it has to constantly expand and monetize, and market, and keep costs down."

"What about in the 90s? How did they do it all back then?"

"Mail. Secret mailing lists and organizations like NAMBLA. They operated along the lines of organized crime, or a gang, or terrorist cell. No one trusts anyone else unless they prove they're committed to the common organization. They'd have gatherings once a member would be vouched for and verified."

"How would they be verified?"

"Some sort of encounter with a child that was taped. Like being made in the Mafia or initiated into a gang. The act had to be captured on tape for proof. Typically stored for blackmail purposes, so the member in question would never rat the others out."

"Mutual destruction," Harri said.

"Something like that," Jackie said and waved for the waitress. Once she'd put in her order, Jackie turned back to Harri. "I heard your sister got caught up in that ring. Do you have any idea of how she was killed?"

"Bullet to the head. It was a through and through. Coroner figures it was 9mm."

"Any leads on her killer?" Jackie asked. "It wasn't the man who died at the island?"

"No. He was one of the victims from the camp. He'd escaped as a child. I only have four generic male names to go by. At least that's what the other victim told me. They only used first names. No one ever slipped up. Only men."

Jackie nodded. "If they're still alive and out there somewhere, I know you'll find them. I know you'll get her killer."

"Even if it kills me," Harri said. "Okay so here's my question."

"Shoot," Jackie said.

"How in this day and age would you go about cracking a child network like that?" Harri asked. She'd read of several networks being busted in the last ten years, and understandably the papers kept it light on the actual investigation. She hoped Jackie could give her some clear insight into the investigative process.

"Oh, boy." Jackie sighed. "Where to start? The last big bust was international, spanning Europe, Canada and the United States. We monitored forums and social media both on the public web and the dark web. Officers also posed as children, engaging with the perpetrators, pretending to be groomed by these individuals who were then tracked by IP address back to their hidey holes on the web and in real life. It's so hard, though. Everything is VPN, which hides the perpetrator's IP address. There's also masking and breadcrumbing where they hide the stuff on a regular blog, or news site. It looks perfectly normal unless you've arrived at that site through a series of links that open the cache of pictures and videos the creeps are looking for."

"So, I'd need to find a computer genius to help me then?" Harri sighed.

"Absolutely. It's all on the internet, now. There are smaller cells that operate like a religious sect. You know, removing themselves from everyday society, then trading the victims around, fostering, re-homing, that sort of thing, but even they communicate over the web."

"What are my chances of finding a bunch of pedophiles in their 60s named John, Paul or George?"

Jackie laughed out loud. "All you're missing is Ringo," Jackie said.

"Ringo? What…" Oh shit, Harri thought. The Beatles. They had used fake names. Now she had even less than nothing.

"They're fake," Harri said.

"I hate to say this but have to be," Jackie frowned. "I

15

read the victim profiles and they wouldn't have taken a chance using their real names. Unless one of the kids overheard a slip."

Harri bit her lip.

"Don't get discouraged, Harri." Jackie continued. "What you could do is go through any witness statements from kids who came forward around that time. They might have more identifying characteristics of their abusers in their written statements that could take you somewhere."

"Even if they aren't the actual guys that were on that island?" Harri asked.

"These guys all know each other," Jackie said, not even trying to hide her disgust. "I don't know what it is. They recognize it in each other. Like it's the way they walk, or some codeword they use. Trust me, all these pervs know each other somehow. Especially in the same general geographical area and if this network was as well-funded as you think it was, pulling any thread of one pedophile from back then should start you down the path to getting the names you need."

"Jake and I've been banging our heads on dead ends. We're both good investigators and we work as a team, but I think we're also too close, you know what I mean?"

"Who's Jake again?"

"Jake Tepesky. He was an FBI profiler at Quantico."

"What's his connection to this case?" Jackie asked.

Harri recognized Jackie's interrogation tone of voice and felt defensive. "He was my sister's best friend," Harri said.

"You guys an item?" Jackie asked with a gleam in her eye, the interrogation tone gone.

"Maybe," Harri said with a small smile.

"Good for you! You need someone to come home to.

Bonus points because he also understands this crazy job."

Harri's smile grew wider. "It's good. It's early and it's good."

The waitress returned with their food and Jackie waited until she'd gone again to continue.

"I can also put you in touch with a friend I have working cybercrime at the FBI once you get on the network's trail."

"I'm not even close to being there yet," Harri said. "My sister's funeral knocked me on my butt. I'd been looking for her for so long and then once I'd found her, I lost the thread a bit. Especially since they'd kept her captive for close to a year."

"I can't imagine what you must be going through with that weighing on you." Jackie shook her head. "Please remember how young you were when she disappeared. A kid. You did everything you could."

Harri nodded. "I know that. I mean, of course I know that. It's just my heart doesn't know it."

Jackie squeezed her hand. "I'm here for you."

"Thank you. I'm hoping I can find something useful to bring to you and your FBI friend."

"I'll help in any way I can. Once a pedo, always a pedo," Jacki said.

"I never stopped looking for her," Harri said.

"And you found her, Harri," Jackie said softly. "You never gave up and you found her."

"Now I'll never stop looking for the men who killed her," Harri said, with a fervor in her voice.

Harri knew she was walking on dangerous ground. These kinds of cases had taken down better detectives than her. Being driven to solve a case walked the fine line between obsession and madness.

"Thank you for meeting with me, Jackie," Harri said.

They'd finished their sandwiches as they talked, and Harri needed to give her two cold cases their due time. Those victims deserved justice, too.

"It was so good to see you, too." Jackie gathered her things. "I need to get going. Gotta get to court," she said.

Harri packed up and followed Jackie out of the diner. Harri hugged her friend good-by and walked back towards the PAB (POLICE ADMINISTRATION BUILD-ING) on Main Street as Jackie headed the opposite direction.

As Harri walked, Robert Payton's last words exploded in her mind.

"I had to make them clean. I had to make them clean," Robert Payton kept repeating as he lay dying.

She wished he'd had a trial and paid for what he'd done to those boys. She could have had a chance to question him. Find out what happened back then, have a sketch artist work with him. Something. Anything.

Bile crept up her esophagus as the enormity of the investigation threatened to overwhelm her. She had to hold the line, keep her head down and focus on each small thread. Each small task. They would get there. Eventually.

She pulled out her badge and stiffened her back. It was time to get to work.

2

DAY 1 – LOS ANGELES, CA

Harri hadn't been sitting at her desk for longer than twenty minutes when she got a call from her lieutenant, Violet Howard, to come to her office. Her heart pounded, and she briefly worried she'd made another misstep. Harri pushed the thought out of her mind as she walked from the Cold Case bullpen to her LT's office.

"You wanted to see me," she asked, then stopped short when she saw an expensively dressed, tall man, with a shock of white hair, sitting across from her LT. Harri didn't know who he was, but he looked like somebody important.

"You wanted to see me, Lieutenant Howard?" she asked again.

"Yes. Detective Harriet Harper, this is Mr. Levi Monroe," the lieutenant said as she motioned to the man who turned and appraised Harri with sharp blue eyes.

"Nice to meet you, Mr. Monroe," she said. Civilians typically didn't show up at the PAB meeting with detectives.

"I saw the work that you did up in Oregon," he started.

Harri shifted on her feet. "Do you have any pertinent information on that case?" Harri asked.

"No, I'm here about my missing daughter," he said.

Harri leaned back against the door frame and gave Violet a quizzical look. Violet pointed to the chair next to Levi Monroe, and Harri peeled herself off the wall and followed the silent command.

"How long has your daughter been missing?" she asked.

"It's been almost four weeks now," Mr. Monroe replied. "She went missing on October nineteenth."

"That's still an open case then," Lieutenant Howard said.

"I want the best for her," Mr. Monroe said. "You found your sister after twenty-five years. If anyone can find my Addy, it will be you."

"I'm sure the detectives on her case are very good and," Harri started, but he held up his hand to stop her.

"They are not taking me seriously. They think she's a runaway and I can't seem to convince them otherwise."

"Mr. Monroe," Harri turned her full attention to the man. "No one understands what you are going through like I do, but you do realize that we are the cold case unit and we typically deal with cases years older than something like this."

"I'm well aware, Detective." Mr. Monroe's tone was dismissive, but then took a determined tone. "I know a great deal more about you than you know about me, so I'll explain. I am a wealthy man. As such, I know most of the power people here in Los Angeles. Am I being understood?" He glanced at the lieutenant and then turned his gaze back to Harri to make sure she was listening.

Harri nodded slightly to indicate he had her full attention and resisted the urge to shoot a look over to her lieutenant.

"Very good," Mr. Monroe continued. "This is a somewhat sensitive case. Addison is my illegitimate daughter. Her mother called me four days ago to tell me she was gone. I want this kept absolutely quiet, and I need her found. She's a good girl and doesn't deserve this."

Harri didn't like his tone or what he wasn't telling them.

"Have you hired private investigators? If you're not happy with the police, then maybe they can help you," Harri suggested.

Lieutenant Howard nodded at that.

"We can't pick up active open cases," Harri explained. "Our cases are years old and open unsolved."

Mr. Monroe sighed and shook his head. "She's only seventeen and I don't believe those detectives have what it takes to find her. I want you, Detective Harper. You are relentless and from everything I've learned about you, driven to find anyone you put your mind to."

He wasn't wrong. Harri had joined the cold case unit because in her search for her sister she had acquired skills and was able to track down people who wanted to stay lost or had gotten lost by misfortune.

She turned to Violet.

"Lieutenant Howard?"

"We really can't be stepping on other detective's toes like this," Violet started.

Mr. Monroe waved her off. "Oh, don't worry about that. I've gone through the proper channels. I've already spoken to your chief. He's given me the go-ahead to bring you onto this case."

"Is he going to inform us himself?" Violet asked.

"I wanted to talk to you first. I need to explain to you about my daughter," Mr. Monroe said. He relaxed into his chair as he spoke. "I couldn't be with her as much as I would have liked. As a father. You understand. However, I monitored her progress and did what I could for her. Addy is an exceptional girl. She's a skilled guitar player. She's extremely talented and has a beautiful voice. She's not lazy. She takes her studies seriously. She's been accepted to Julliard on a full scholarship. She has no idea that I actually arranged that, and she still had to apply, you see. She still had to compete for it, and she won it."

"How did you arrange the scholarship?" Harri asked.

"I created it," Mr. Monroe explained. "When she showed her musical aptitude at such a young age, I created the scholarship so that she could eventually use it to further her studies. But you see, she knows nothing of that and she would never run away from that opportunity. You must understand, she's worked her entire life to be in a position where she could study and become the absolute best. I knew she would, because no matter what, she is a Monroe at the end of the day. Disappearing without any word to anyone is not like her and it drives her mother and me absolutely insane to hear people dismiss her as just some dumb, reckless teenager."

"I'm sure those detectives haven't dismissed her," Violet began.

"Those incompetent detectives don't matter anymore. This is Detective Harper's case now and I know she will not disappoint us."

With that said, he rubbed his palms on his knees and stood up. He really was a tall and imposing man, Harri thought.

"Detective." He gave Harri a nod. "I will make myself available to you for any questions you might have. I assure you I won't be one of those fathers who calls every day to check on the case, though. I can call the chief for that."

That was even worse than a frantic parent calling several times a day, Harri thought. Her big plan of keeping a low profile and not sticking her neck out to be noticed had just been shot to shit. There was no way she wouldn't be eyeballed now, especially on a case that had just been yanked out of someone else's hands, and especially when the father was so well-connected.

"I'll wait for the chief's call then," Lieutenant Howard said.

"Thank you so much for coming in Mr. Monroe." Harri stood and shook his hand.

He nodded again and left, his perfectly polished black shoes clicking as he walked over the wooden floor towards the outer doors of the cold case unit. Only after they'd heard the door open and close to the hallway outside, did Harri and Violet speak.

"What did we just get into?" she asked.

"Extra analysis on how we do our jobs, that's for sure," Violet said. "Can you handle a case like this? With the surveillance from above?"

"I wish I didn't have to," Harri said truthfully.

"Are you still not sleeping at night?" Violet picked up a pen and twirled it between her fingers. Harri recognized it as the lieutenant's go to when she was brainstorming.

Harri had been putting in extra overtime for the last

three weeks, even though she wasn't getting much done and Violet had noticed. Violet noticed everything in her unit.

"I'm much better," Harri lied. "I'm back and even though it's been a slow start for me, I can handle this." She didn't think she could handle it, but if she could convince Violet, maybe she could convince herself.

"And he involved the Chief of Police," Violet tossed the pen on the desk in disgust.

"Have you ever had one of these cases before? A powerful parent bringing something like this to our department?"

"You know that's not how it works." Violet shook her head. "Ever. I'll wait for the chief to call and notify me we're officially on this case. Until then, I'll make sure to get the files so you can start."

"Who were the detectives?" she asked.

"I know one of them was Jorge Hernandez," Violet said.

Harri knew Jorge Hernandez from the Creek Killer task force. He was a good, thorough detective and she doubted he'd been dismissive of Addison's disappearance as her father claimed.

"Jorge is good," she said.

"I know." Violet nodded. "Look, these super wealthy people just want what they want and they'll pull any string to get it."

"Lucky me." Harri sighed.

"Lucky Addison." Violet nodded and shuffled some papers on her desk.

Harri was dismissed. She wandered back to her desk and sat down, feeling weary even though the day was barely half done. She stared at the files of the two cases she'd made no progress on and bit her lip.

Harri needed to get it together to find this girl. She closed her eyes and imagined her sister on that last day, so hopeful about going on a hike in the woods. Another girl was missing. Her entire life in front of her. Just like her sister. She would find her. This time she would find her in time.

3

DAY 1

J ake Tepesky sat at his kitchen table looking out over the hills toward the Hollywood sign. It was an impressive view and one that usually calmed him. Today wasn't one of those days.

He sipped his coffee and shuffled through the file that Harri and he'd put together on Jerome Wexler, the man whose name was on the lease for Black Rock Island, the site of Nightwood Camp.

The camp had been a front for a child pornography operation and served as a remote location where pedophiles went to abuse boys. Harri's older sister, Lauren Harper, had been murdered there along with nine other children twenty-five years ago. Both Harri and Jake vowed to discover who'd ordered their deaths and the men who had carried them out.

Lauren's remains had taken weeks to be released and they'd finally been able to hold a funeral at the end of October, close to twenty-five years to when she'd originally gone missing.

Since then, they'd channeled their grief by immediately getting to work. Jake searched through numerous databases for Jerome Wexler's current whereabouts. Harri had done the same and so far, both had come up empty. The man had become a ghost, vanishing in the wind.

They'd also searched for John, Paul, and George, the men that Richard Miller had named as the ones who'd herded all the kids out of the camp that last night. They'd had no luck finding any leads on them, either. There was just too little to go on.

Harri had pored through arrest records for the entire Pacific Northwest for known pedophiles and child pornographers with those names or aliases but had come up empty. No men matching their ages or names showed up in the records. They had no descriptions to follow up on.

Jake wasn't as sure as Harri about the names of the men anyway. He believed they used aliases. Harri thought they felt safe enough to use their real names. The pedophiles had chosen and groomed their victims well. They never expected for any of the boys to speak out against them. Who would believe them?

Lauren was a whole other story, though. That's where Harri's argument about the real names fell apart. There was no way the perpetrators would have used their real names around Lauren, and adult woman who wouldn't hesitate to testify against them.

Jake had always been a proponent of trying every direction on a case to see what would turn up. The arrest records were just the basic first steps. The money trail tended to show more results. When he turned in that direction, things went weird.

Jerome Wexler emptied his accounts soon after he fled the country, just before the joint task force could arrest him on charges of child endangerment and child pornography. It was an understandable move on Wexler's part, but Jake was surprised at how quickly he was able to do it. Even before Homeland Security came into being and the banking laws changed on large cash withdrawals, cashing out that big was not easy. Wexler had been able to liquidate almost immediately. Jake was thankful that he was looking at twenty-five-year-old data. The good thing was there was a trail. The bad thing was that it was incomplete. If the situation was current, there would hardly be a trail at all, as everything would be offshore accounts over the internet.

The larger mystery appeared when Jake went searching for how Wexler made his money and where he came from. He struggled to put together a dossier they could use to track family, acquaintances, and close associates to Jerome Wexler's current location. What Harri and Jake discovered though, was that Jerome Wexler didn't exist before 1985.

Wexler made a big splash in 1987 when he turned up as the main financial advisor to one of the wealthiest men in the Pacific Northwest.

Reginald Smith had founded the Regional Hardware franchise with dozens of locations throughout Washington, Oregon and even Northern California and Idaho. Reginald had made millions upon millions through the stores and Jerome Wexler managed his entire fortune. Wexler had sole discretion on buying and selling company stock, as well as other lucrative investments and trade transactions. Within that first year, Jerome acquired a portfolio of expensive properties throughout the Pacific Northwest. When Jake spoke to his contacts in the finance industry, he uncovered what looked to be

Wexler's siphoning off of Reginald's money into his own private accounts.

Unfortunately for them, Reginald Smith was long dead with no surviving family. Regional Hardware had been chopped up and sold off more than a decade ago. This was just one of the difficulties investigating long cold cases. Some trails just disappeared into thin air. Reginald Smith's and Jerome Wexler's money trail definitely had.

When they turned to looking into how Jerome Wexler had left the country right after that fateful night, they hit another roadblock. Jake dug up flight manifests from a private airstrip outside of Portland, Oregon. It was where Wexler kept his private jet and supposedly flew to Europe to escape prosecution. The manifest indicated they were headed to the Netherlands. Convenient the Netherlands doesn't have an extradition treaty with the United States. Jerome Wexler had chosen well.

Jake reached far into his contacts to find someone at the National Central Bureau (Interpol) at the Hague. After three different officers, he'd finally found someone who might be able to help and he was anxiously waiting on the call back.

The frustration at the flight manifest not panning out still caused Jake's neck to tighten up. It'd taken him a week of digging through dusty, old boxes to even find the records for that flight. At the time, he'd thought he'd struck gold. Then he found Jerome Wexler had dropped off the face of the earth. If Wexler was still alive, he must have used his money and power to buy a completely brand-new identity.

His cellphone buzzed and he grabbed it. "Jake Tepesky speaking," he said. A crackle came through before a distorted voice screeched in feedback and Jake pulled his ear away from the phone, waiting until the line settled.

"Officer Jan DeVries speaking," the voice said on the other line.

Jake looked down at the name he'd been given by his friend Jerry who worked at the Hague and confirmed DeVries was the name of the contact.

"Thanks so much for getting back to me, Officer DeVries," Jake said.

"I hear you have an old one for me," he said. His voice was bright and cheery with a thick Dutch accent ending each sentence with a light lilt.

"It is an old one. A known pornographer named Jerome Wexler took a private jet to the Netherlands in 1994," Jake explained. "I'm searching for his current whereabouts. My contact Jerry Blyth did a preliminary scan and found no individual by that name currently living in the Netherlands. I wanted to know if Jerome Wexler might have crossed your radar? Might be during any investigations into human trafficking or pornography rings?"

He heard a shuffling of papers on the other end.

"I ran Jerome Wexler through our archives going back to 1994, DeVries replied." Jerry provided me the information for this phone call. Unfortunately, I found no mention of this individual in cases either open or closed. That doesn't mean that he is not here, but if so, he's been a good quiet citizen."

"That's hard to believe because these men never give up that kind of work."

"I agree," DeVries said. "Would you by chance have any other aliases that he used in the states?"

"Unfortunately, I don't. Jerome Wexler is all I have."

"Here is the interesting thing that I found," Officer

DeVries said.

"Interesting in a good way or in a bad way?" Jake asked.

"I spoke with immigration and did some digging of my own through the necessary channels here in the Netherlands and we don't have any records of a Jerome Wexler arriving in the country on any date."

"Did the private jet land at any of your Airports of Entry? He'd have to have gone through customs. One of those airports would have records?"

"I checked all of those airports. Luckily, we computerized the records going back that far. That private jet never landed in this country."

Jake's shoulders slumped. He'd fully hit a dead end.

"Thank you so much for all of this information. It's disappointing, but I really appreciate your closing the loop on this part of the investigation," Jake said.

"I'm sorry I couldn't give you more helpful information," Officer DeVries said.

"One more question. Have you uncovered any major human trafficking or child abuse rings in the Netherlands?"

"As you can imagine, I cannot speak to open cases and active investigations," DeVries said. "Speaking more generally, most of the human trafficking right now is coming out of the Middle East and Syria. There are several ongoing child pornography ring cases going on at Interpol currently. You'd need to speak to my colleague in the Cyber Crime division. Would you like her number?" he asked.

"Please. I'd really like to speak to her," he said.

Officer DeVries gave him the contact information for an Annika Stoop. Jake thanked him again and hung up.

The pit formed in the bottom of his stomach and

exhaustion flowed from his head down to his toes. He'd been so hopeful those flight manifests would lead to something major and he'd come up empty. He breathed in deep and tried to swallow the frustration that welled up once again.

This criminal was going to be difficult to find, he thought. Difficult, but not impossible. Jake knew Harri would never stop looking for Jerome Wexler and he cared too much about Harri to let her track him down alone. Lauren never deserved to have her life end that way. Jake owed it to Lauren to help Harri bring Jerome Wexler justice.

He got up from the table and put his coffee cup into the sink. He looked over at the files piled up on the table, trying to decide whether he could use another coffee or if it would make him too jittery to work. He'd checked his email earlier that morning and had two consultation cases in his mailbox.

As a former Quantico profiler, he typically freelanced with police departments to help them on tough cases. He'd taken a two-month break from the work to help Harri find Lauren. When they discovered her remains, he put together the funeral and handled whatever business that Harri couldn't.

He liked his work and didn't need the money. He had enough stashed away. Truth be told, his job kept his own dark thoughts at bay. If he didn't have the work, he wouldn't get out of bed.

Depression had hit him hard after all the cases he'd profiled. One of the reasons he had quit. He could no longer compartmentalize all the horror. He turned back to his computer. Harri wouldn't like the news on this lead. At least he had another contact to call. If Jerome Wexler was still alive, they would track him down.

4

DAY 1

J uliet Adamson excitedly ran up the walk of the Hollywood Hills home that her and her boyfriend Roger had rented for the weekend. It was her birthday and he'd sprung the surprise on her which she loved him for.

They lived in a small one-bedroom apartment in the middle of Hollywood. The cramped apartment was stuffy and hot. Frankly it just wasn't very romantic. She wanted to turn thirty in style and spending it in a Hollywood Hills designer home was just the thing to perk up her mood.

Roger found the keys in the key box hanging on the statue of a dog to the left of the front door.

"Cute layout," Juliet remarked.

Roger grinned. "Let's hope this place is as cool as advertised."

He opened the door and stood back. "Ladies first."

Juliet rolled her eyes and stepped into the foyer. The house smelled musty and lived in. She wrinkled her nose.

"Ew. Gross. What's that smell?"

Roger was right behind her and sniffed. "We need to open all the windows." He dropped their bags to the side of the door and went around the living room opening up the windows.

She walked over to the French doors leading out to the backyard and squealed in delight.

"There's a pool," she cried. "There's a pool. Roger, you did such a good job getting this place." She grabbed him and planted a big fat kiss on his lips.

"I aim to please," he said and went in for more.

She pushed back from his embrace. "You smell that?" she asked.

There was a different smell now and it wasn't musty and stale. It smelled foul, like something had died in the wall.

They crossed through the kitchen into the dining room and noticed a damp brown patch on the bottom of the back wall. The sheetrock had peeled off in that corner. Something had cracked through the brittle interior of the sheetrock.

"Oh God. I do smell that," Roger said. "Something died in that wall,"

"We should call the owner," she said, covering her nose and mouth with her hand.

Roger dialed their B&B host. The call went to voicemail.

"We can't stay here," she said.

Roger groaned. He'd spent a lot of money on this surprise. "What if we open up the wall? Get the dead animal out of there so the smell can clear out. Tom has that cleaning company. I'm sure he could come and clean it today so we can enjoy your birthday weekend," Roger said.

"The B&B host should be doing that," she whined. This was her birthday weekend and she didn't want to be dealing with something gross like this.

"I know, babe." Roger sighed. "It's a solution, though. He's not picking up and we can tell him that we did him a favor and he could clean it up after we leave," Roger said.

"Okay." Juliet nodded. "How are we going to rip this wall open?" she asked as she went back to the living room and rummaged in her bag to find a scarf to put over her face.

Roger headed to the kitchen. He opened drawers and cabinets until he found what he was looking for.

He walked back to her waving a hammer.

"That's what you are going to use?" she asked skeptically as she wrapped the scarf around her neck to cover her nose and mouth.

"I'm strong, baby." He flexed his biceps and grinned. "I got the muscles," he said and got to work.

"Wait." Juliet followed him back to the dining room and the rotted smell.

Roger turned back to her and she put a rolled-up tank top around his neck to cover his nose and mouth. It was pink and he flinched as she tied it in the back.

"Stop it," Juliet said. "No one's gonna see you. There could be mold in there."

It only took two good swings of the hammer for the damaged sheetrock to give way. After he opened a good four-foot opening, he peered inside.

"There's plastic in here," he said.

The smell of death filled the air. Juliet swallowed her rising bile. She was going to puke if she stayed in the room.

She ran over to the kitchen windows and threw them

open to get more fresh air. This was turning out to be a lot worse than just a dead rat. There was no way that smell was something small.

"Oh shit," she heard Roger say. She watched as he scrambled away from the hole. That didn't bode well.

"What is it?" She called from the kitchen, afraid of his answer. "A raccoon? Or?" Even though the words had left her mouth she already knew it wasn't a dead animal.

It was a dead body. There was no way around it.

Juliet had watched enough real-crime documentary shows and missing person news segments with her mother to know they had stumbled across a dead body. She watched Roger as he watched her pull her cell phone from her purse.

"911 what is your emergency?"

"Hi," Juliet began and then hesitated.

"Hello? What is your emergency?"

"We found a dead body in the wall." The words came out louder and faster than she intended.

Roger rushed to her side and grabbed the phone.

"Hello, are you there? What is the address?"

Roger held her hand as he gave the 911 operator the address of their B&B.

Juliet stared at the hole in the wall as Roger spoke to the 911 operator. She might not be getting her romantic birthday weekend, but it would definitely be something interesting to talk about.

5

DAY 1

Debi Mills sat in the casting office with six other girls who looked like they could be her twin. She was waiting for her turn to audition for a web commercial for a software company she'd never heard of. Her agent kept sending her out on commercial auditions because she had the girl-next-door look they always wanted, but she also had the strawberry-red hair that gave her a quirky look that was all the rage right now.

Unfortunately, her natural shade seemed to have been readily available in the box because five of the girls that sat in the cramped waiting room looked exactly like her all the way down to the bangs.

She nervously glanced to the side and then casually around the room. She had her lines memorized and repeated them in her mind to distract her from the other girls in the room. It was a high-energy commercial about a girl who had just gotten her new computer and was thanking her parents for her birthday gift.

Debi was seventeen, but looked more like fourteen

and her agent said she was a shoo-in for this specific casting director. Marguerite liked the younger actresses coming in too, he added.

A girl came out of the side door looking pretty upset. An audition gone bad, Debi thought. The young actress looked like the rest of the girls in the waiting room. She hurried past everyone to the exit as an assistant peeked her head out of the same door and called another girl's name.

One of her doppelgängers stood up and followed the woman inside. Debi just couldn't believe how many girls there were that looked exactly like her.

That was the key to commercials. They were looking for a type. The funny one, the girl next door, the sexpot, the mom, some stereotype that could immediately be telegraphed.

At least that's what her agent, August, told her. She trusted him and hoped that was the right choice to make. She was as street smart as a kid could be coming out of the suburbs of Arizona.

She had come to Los Angeles two years ago at the age of fifteen as a runaway. Her mother was an opioid addict and her father had been in prison for so long she couldn't even remember the last time she saw him. After the last time her mother nearly overdosed and died, Debi knew she had to get away. She took off, taking a Greyhound bus from Arizona to Los Angeles.

It had been a tough first year, but she'd come with a plan. She found a room right away in a charity house for runaway teens. There she met a girl who helped her get extras work on tv shows with live audiences. She met August Jackson at one of those gigs. He became her agent.

She hadn't booked any real commercials yet, but she

was getting a lot of auditions. It was just a matter of time. August helped her get a fake ID stating she was twenty-one so she could waitress. She'd sent out her headshots to all five of the places he'd recommended. The fifth one said yes. It was a diner in Echo Park that had open mic comedy nights. She was able to find a room in a house a few blocks from the diner.

It wasn't glamorous, but at least she didn't have to watch her mother waste away from her addiction. It was a tough life, but it was her own.

She looked down at the lines again and wished she'd get called already. A waft of expensive perfume made her look up. A well-dressed woman in her thirties with a dark bob had taken the seat next to her. Their eyes met and the woman gave Debi a warm smile.

"Are you ready for this?" she asked.

"As ready as I'll ever be," Debi said.

"When's it your turn?" the woman asked.

"My audition was for three o'clock," Debi said and looked at the time. It was already four o'clock. Why did all the auditions have to always run late?

"They do always run late, don't they?" The woman echoed Debi's thoughts.

"God, yes. Why is that?"

"It's always been like that. Are you new?" the woman asked.

"I've been at it for a couple of years," Debi admitted. She was surprised she'd told her that. Debi wasn't so into talking to strangers.

"You look young," the woman asked.

"I think that's why I'm getting so many auditions," Debi said without thinking.

"Because of how young you look? How old are you?" the woman asked.

"I'm seventeen."

"I would've never put you past fourteen," the woman said. "Are you getting a lot of callbacks?"

"I am. Mostly for girl-next-door type for commercials," Debi admitted.

"Your age helps that since you can work longer hours than a fourteen-year-old," the woman said.

Debi nodded and wondered why she was talking to her. Some other girls were glancing her way with jealousy in their eyes. She must be someone important. That made Debi sit up straighter.

"My name is Georgie," the woman held her hand out to Debi. "Georgie Shipwell."

"My name is Debi Mills, nice to meet you," Debi said as she shook her hand. "Are you a casting director here?"

"Oh no," Georgie said. "I'm here to see Marguerite. She's a dear friend of mine. We're supposed to grab an early dinner. It looks like she's going to be late though."

"Yes, we still have four girls left," Debi said and looked over at the girls still reading their sides.

One of them shot her a dirty look and looked away. Debi was happy to be chatting with Georgie. It was helping her nerves.

"Are you new in town?" Georgie asked.

"Why would you ask that?" Debi asked in surprise.

"You seem so fresh," Georgie said. She leaned closer to Debi and lowered her voice. "And Los Angeles can kind of wear a girl down if you know what I mean," she said.

"I came here two years ago," Debi said.

"Why did your parents move here?"

"I moved here myself," Debi said and didn't expound on the reason why. Georgie smiled brightly. "I do hope you get it. I'll put in a good word for you with

Marguerite. Be good to have some fresh faces in these commercials that you see."

Debi nodded and smiled. Could this be the break she was looking for? It couldn't be that easy, could it? She'd heard stories about girls being plucked out of obscurity and getting their careers rolling just like this. And this wasn't some guy that would want to try to have sex with her. It was a woman which is so nice because a lot of times women just didn't want to help other women. Georgie didn't seem like she was that kind of woman, though.

The door opened again, and another girl came out. The blonde-haired woman peeked her head out and took note of the remaining girls in the room. When she caught sight of Georgie, she smiled.

"Georgie, I'm so glad you came. I'm going to be so late," Marguerite said. "Come inside," she waved her over.

Georgie stood up and smiled down at Debi." Nice to meet you. Best of luck," she said and sauntered over to Marguerite where they air-kissed and gave each other hugs.

The door closed and Debi went back to her sides. She was having trouble concentrating on her lines now, as her mind raced at all the possibilities this first job could potentially open for her. Oh, she did hope that Georgie would put in a good word with Marguerite for her.

Her heart skipped a beat and her cheeks flushed.

A little jolt of happiness found a home in her chest. She had endured so much in her short life and she would be so grateful to finally catch a break. It was her time and if she did manage to book this job, she knew all the others would soon follow.

That's what August always said. It just takes that one job and then they were off to the races.

He was in a small agency out in the valley and was trying to make a name for himself, too. It's probably why he was sending her to so many auditions.

Debi was grateful for his support and wanted to prove to him and herself that she could and would be a successful actress.

If just given a chance.

The door opened again, and another girl was called. Debi took a deep breath and lifted up her chin.

Today was going to be her day.

6

DAY 1

Detective Harri Harper pulled up to a modest bungalow in the Los Feliz area of Los Angeles. Los Feliz was one of those neighborhoods that eighteen years ago was working class. Now it was filled with million-dollar homes nestled between smaller bungalows whose residents had lived in them for over thirty years when it was a gang-infested hood.

It was a strange eclectic mix of the upwardly mobile and the working class. Mavis James's home looked more working class than the million-dollar homes surrounding hers.

Harri grabbed her purse, her notebook, and her phone and walked up to the front door. She knocked and a woman in her forties opened it a crack. Her eyes were puffy and her skin blotchy. She'd been recently crying.

"May I help you?" she asked.

"My name is Detective Harriet Harper," Harri said. "I've been tasked to help find your daughter, Addison. I'm not sure if you've already spoken with my colleagues?"

"I'm so glad you're here," she whimpered and gestured for Harri to come inside.

Harri stepped into the darkened hallway and walked into a small living room furnished with couch, chair, coffee table and a flat-screen TV on the wall. Mavis James was not interested in decorating, apparently. The furniture was purely functional.

"Please sit," Mavis James said and motioned to the couch.

Harri sat down and Mavis joined her on the other end.

"If you don't find a missing person in the first forty-eight hours, they're most likely gone for good," Mavis began.

"That does not necessarily have to be the case. Especially with teenagers who have the tendency to run..."

"Addy did not run away," Mavis said in a weary voice. As if she'd said that same thing a thousand times already.

"How can you be so sure?" Harri asked.

She knew the question came off as blunt, but it was easier to get to the bottom of whatever family dynamics were happening. Addy had already been gone for three weeks and Harri needed to cut to the chase.

"We didn't have problems like that." Mavis shook her head as if she already knew what Harri was going to say. "Addy didn't run away. She had just started seeing a boy and he is kind and nice. She has her guitar here and, quite frankly, if she had run away, she would've taken her guitar with her."

"Addison's father mentioned that she had a full ride to Julliard?" Harri asked.

"That's correct." Mavis nodded. "She's going to start next fall. They wanted her to come early because of how exceptional she is, but she decided she wanted to finish up her senior year at John Marshall."

"John Marshall was her high school?" Harri asked, jotting it down in her notebook.

"Yes," Mavis said and sniffled.

"When was the last time you saw your daughter?" Harri asked. She got out her phone and activated the voice recorder. "You don't mind if I record this, do you?"

Mavis shook her head no. She was an attractive blonde with creamy skin who could easily still have men turning their heads as she walked by. She'd caught a slight scent of alcohol and body odor from Mavis. As if she hadn't showered in a day and drank herself to numbness instead. Harri wondered what she did for a living, but she knew that wasn't a pertinent question yet.

"I saw her on her way to school," Mavis said carefully, so as not to start crying again. "It was a Friday and she went off at the normal time. She doesn't have any guitar lessons on Friday, so she left her guitar at home. She'd mentioned to me she was staying over at Sophie Lambert's house that night."

"And Sophie Lambert is her friend?"

"Her best friend actually." Mavis smiled. "Since they were little girls. She's trying to be an actor. I kept telling her that it's a grueling profession and not worth all the sacrifices you have to make for it, but she doesn't listen. She's got the bug."

Harri nodded and jotted down that Mavis James was a former actor.

"And does she typically go anywhere without her cell phone?" Harri asked. That was one of the things she'd discovered as she started looking to the case. "Addy's cell phone was found at Sophie Lambert's house. Knowing teenagers, that doesn't make a lick of sense."

"Never." Mavis shook her head. "I know that if she left it at Sophie's, it was by accident."

The other detectives must've told Mavis about the phone.

"Did Addy and Sophie have any problems recently?" Harri asked. She jotted down that she would need to be seeing Sophie Lambert next.

"No." Mavis shook her head. "Thick as thieves, those two. If there was a snit, I would have known it. She's missing too, you know," Mavis said.

"Has she been reported missing by her parents?" Harri asked.

Harri struggled to keep her composure and not alarm Mavis James. This was new information to her. Nothing in the files mentioned that Sophie Lambert was also missing. How could Jorge Hernandez have missed that? He couldn't have, Harri knew. He wasn't the best detective on the force, but he knew better than that. He was no rookie. Something was wrong, but Harri filed it away for the moment.

"Of course, she was," Mavis insisted. "Elle Lambert, that's her mother, is a full-blown stage mom. Sophie was constantly being pulled out of school for auditions. There is no way that Elle would let a single day go by without knowing where her daughter was."

"So both girls went missing Friday night?" Harri asked.

Mavis nodded and put her hand on her own throat, to stop the threatening tears from coming again.

"And where did Elle Lambert think Sophie was?"

"Here, if you can believe it." Mavis shook her head. "The oldest trick in the book. Each girl telling their parents they're at the other's house. Hard to imagine parents still fall for that crap," Mavis said as tears sprouted in her eyes again. "But I did."

"And what is Addison's boyfriend's name?"

"Nick Young. He also goes to Marshall High."

Harri jotted down more notes as she gave Mavis James time to compose herself. Teenagers were always running away, but this didn't feel like one of those cases. Harri thought about Addison's father, Levi Monroe. He and Mavis were right. Their daughter was extraordinary, but every teenager could have a reason to run. Something about this case so far didn't add up. Harri could feel it.

"Can you please show me Addison's room?" Harri asked.

Mavis got up and led Harri to a room down the hall. "I've kept it exactly as it was that day. Just like the other detective told me."

Harri looked into a bedroom painted baby blue. Where Mavis had neglected decorating with any warmth or cheer, Addison had surrounded herself with an explosion of color and femininity. Harri glanced around the room and noted the white painted furniture, white metal-frame bed, the patterned bed cover and pillows and the guitars. Three of them, two were in cases.

Harri nodded and closed the door. She followed Mavis back to the sofa where they both sat again.

"Have you put up flyers in the neighborhood?" Harri asked. "Talked to her friends? Checked her social media?"

Mavis wiped a tear and waved her hand dismissively. "All of that. I've done everything that other detective suggested. I've posted flyers and posted in the mom groups on Facebook, but nobody has seen her. She's just vanished."

"I'll do whatever it takes to find her," Harri said before she could stop herself.

"Please find my baby," Mavis said and burst into tears again.

Harri reached out and took Mavis' hand in hers. "I will do my best." Harri assured her.

"I gave Levi your name. I read all about how you found your sister up in Oregon. After twenty-five years. If you could find her in the woods, you can find my daughter in this goddamn city."

Harri nodded again. "I never give up."

Mavis wiped her tears with a linen handkerchief. Harri saw the same monogram of Levi Monroe's that was on the card he'd left with Lt. Violet Howard.

"I'll be in touch as soon as I have any information," Harri said as she gathered her purse and heaved herself off the couch.

Mavis nodded meekly and began to stand.

"Don't worry. I'll see myself out," Harri said.

Relieved, Mavis fell back into the sofa.

As Harri passed by her, she caught another whiff of light body odor and a lot of alcohol mixed together. Mavis was in the same kind of pain that her mother and father had endured when Lauren had gone missing.

Harri placed her hand to her chest and rushed out of the house. Gulping for air, she ran away from Mavis' pain and didn't stop moving until she was in her car.

As she started the car, her mind played through the interview. She had to speak with Jorge Hernandez next because the investigation into Addison's and Sophie's disappearances didn't make any sense to her. Whenever a detective took a case over from another detective, there was an exchange of information. She'd tried reaching him before she'd left for this interview but, he was out in the field and unavailable.

Her cell phone interrupted her thoughts. When she looked at the number, she didn't recognize it. She answered it anyway.

"Detective Harper speaking," she said.

"Hi Harri, Tom Bards here."

Harri frowned. Detective Tom Bards worked in the Robbery Homicide Division. She'd worked with him on the Creek killer case back in September but hadn't crossed paths with him since. As far as she'd heard, they were still down at that ranch digging through evidence.

Harri pulled into the traffic on her way back to the PAB. "Detective Bards, what can I do for you?" she asked.

"Seems we have intersecting cases," he replied.

"Please don't tell me you've found Addison James?" Harri said, biting her lip.

"Actually, no," Bards said. "We do have a body, but we've identified it as a Sophie Lambert," he said.

"Her best friend." Harri sighed. "Where was she found?"

"In the wall of some B&B off Beachwood Canyon. You anywhere near there?" he asked.

"I can be. Are you there?" she asked.

"I am and I've been given the go-ahead to bring you onto this seeing as you're working the Addison James case."

"Really?" She couldn't help but ask. Lieutenant Richard Byrne ran the Robbery Homicide Division and they were mortal enemies. Tom Bards must've moved mountains to get her attached to an RHD case. The RHD was famous for taking high-profile and media-heavy cases. It was the elite of elite detectives and a full-on boys club ruled over by one Lieutenant Richard Byrne.

Byrne had tried to push her off the Creek Killer task force even though she'd been instrumental in bringing those killers to justice by finding the woman calling herself Jane Smith.

She'd left on decent terms with the detectives she worked with, but after her escapades in Oregon she thought any hope she'd have of taking a crack at getting into RHD was long gone. Just as well because she found the cold cases suited her. And now, Detective Tom Bards was giving her a chance again.

"On my way from Los Feliz," she said.

Tom gave her the address and she put it into her navigation app on her phone. Her heart raced as the adrenaline of getting a new case filled her. The news of Sophie's death didn't bode well for Addison still being alive. But with a body, they had clues. There'd be records of people in that home. A lead.

As she drove, Harri almost felt like herself again. Back on a case. Focused on helping find someone's loved one and bringing a killer to justice.

She'd had a hard time since Lauren's funeral. She and Jake had struck out on every lead so far in trying to locate Jerome Wexler, the man she felt was responsible for Lauren's murder. She had a low frustration threshold recently. Working cases made her feel like her old self again. This is good, she thought. This is what I'm supposed to be doing. This is where I'm supposed to be, she thought as she sped to the location.

7

DAY 1

It took Harri only fifteen minutes to get to the address Detective Tom Bards had given her. She pulled up behind several police cruisers and the coroner's van. She flashed her badge to the uniform standing behind the yellow crime scene tape at the end of the long drive.

"Is Detective Tom Bards inside?" she asked.

The uniform nodded. She ducked under the tape and climbed up the steep driveway. She stepped into the house and found Detective Tom Bards in the living room talking with the coroner.

Dr. Leanne Grimley turned toward Harri and smiled.

"Detective Harper. So glad to see you. My condolences on your sister."

"May she finally rest in peace," Tom said.

"Thank you so much, Dr. Grimley. Detective Bards. That means a lot."

They stood awkwardly for a beat and then got to business.

"Have we made a positive ID as Sophie Lambert?" Harri asked. She'd been surprised by the fast ID.

"One of the uniformed officers showed me the missing person photo when we opened up the plastic sheeting and saw her face," Tom explained. "He'd been called out on the original missing person's call, I guess."

"She was a very distinctive looking young lady," Dr. Grimley said.

"Distinctive how?" Harri asked.

"She looks a lot like Megan Fox," Tom said.

"The actress Megan Fox?" Harri asked.

"A younger version of her. Sophie Lambert was only seventeen and looked it," Tom said.

"How did you connect her with Addison James? I didn't see her name in Addison's file," Harri asked.

"They didn't connect the two girls initially," Tom replied. "When we called her parents to make the official ID, her mother asked if we'd also found Addison James."

Dr. Grimley left them to talk as she worked on the body.

"How did you know that I was on the Addison James case?" she asked.

"Everybody knows you're on that case, Harri."

And by everyone, he meant Richard Byrne. It must really chap his hide to know that Harri Harper, disgraced girl cop as he'd once called her, was investigating another prominent case after all he'd done to try tanking her career.

"Thank you for calling me on this. I just finished interviewing Addison James' mother right before you called, and Mavis James is positive the girls disappeared together."

"That's Elle Lambert's take on it, too."

"She have any idea where they were going?" she asked.

"She was supposed to be at Addison James' house." Tom shook his head. "The old crisscross."

"That is precisely why I am happy not to have children," Harri said under her breath.

Tom nodded without a word.

"Do you have a cause of death?"

"Too early to tell. From Grimley's initial review of the body, there are no apparent signs of violence. The body was in advanced decomp so that's not saying much. She's scheduling the autopsy for the next available."

"How long has she been dead?"

"Grimley says four days," Tom said.

"She was kept somewhere for the last three weeks? The girls went missing on October 18th. It's now almost Thanksgiving."

"It appears that way," he said.

"Is this the scene of the murder?" she asked. "Who found her?"

"A couple who was supposed to be spending the weekend here. It's a B&B rental, much to the delight of the neighbors. They all call it the party house."

"Does the host have a record of who stayed here four days ago?" she asked.

"Their records show the place was empty. Paul Lancel, the owner, says he has no idea how she got into the wall. He hasn't been on site for over a month. Doesn't mean much as the key is right outside the door. Any guest who knew the code could get in."

"No wonder his neighbors hate him," Harri said dryly.

"Makes me never want to stay in a B&B," Tom said.

"Are you thinking this is the primary crime scene? Any signs of a struggle?" Harri asked.

"I'm thinking no," Tom said. "I don't have proof of that, though. Just a hunch."

"How did RHD get this case anyway?" Harri asked, curious. Sophie wasn't someone famous and wouldn't garner too much media attention. There were a lot of seventeen-year-old girls who disappeared from Los Angeles every day.

"It's her connection to Addison James, I think. Now that there's a body and daddy is so connected, they decided to call in RHD."

Harri nodded and turned back to the activity going past the kitchen. "How do you want to work this? Do we talk to the parents next?" she asked. "Do I stay on Addison?"

"We're formally interviewing them tomorrow. They're coming in tonight to make the official ID. I don't think I need you there for that." Tom glanced at his watch. "Listen, it's already almost five. Maybe it's better for you to start fresh tomorrow morning. We can go together to their house for the interview."

Harri liked the sound of that and nodded. "Happy to be working with you again, Tom," she said.

"Likewise," he said.

"See you in the morning," she said and waved to Grimley, who was hunched over the body.

"See you soon," Dr. Grimley called out.

Harri climbed into her car and texted Jake Tepesky to tell him she was on her way. It was her turn to stay over at his place.

As she drove to Jake's house, her thoughts scrambled

through the day's events. Getting the Addison James case just like that and then having Sophie Lambert's body turn up. It was almost too much of a coincidence, but it happened.

Harri felt the adrenaline kicking into gear. She hadn't felt this way about the cold cases she'd been assigned when she returned to work. This case, however, had struck a chord. Teenage girls gone missing. Like her sister.

There was hope she'd find Addison still alive. They'd kept Sophie for weeks. If they could find her in time, another life could be saved. A family taken from the brink of despair.

She pulled onto Jake's street within minutes. She hadn't realized how close he lived to the party house.

8

DAY 1 -NIGHT

Harri pulled into the little parking space in front of Jake's home. She grabbed her purse and locked up the car. Looking ruefully up the massive set of stairs, she sighed. Jake's home was perched on top of a canyon and the only way to get to his front door was up four flights of very steep stairs.

Harri hated those stairs.

She grunted and started on the first set. Even though they were splitting time between her home and his, it would be so much easier if he came to hers. She didn't have stairs.

Better yet, he might as well move in. Even though they'd only been together since Oregon, which was a month plus some days, she'd known him all her life.

Harri was prepared to take the next step with him. She thought he was ready as well, but she was too afraid to broach the subject with him.

Because it had only been a month.

But boy, did she not want to do these stairs again. She

trudged up one flight and then another flight and had to stop to catch her breath.

Damn these stairs. Her thighs burning, she ran up the last flight of stairs, her breath coming out in short gasps. The door opened as she hit the last stair. Jake stood silhouetted in the doorway. She could make out a grin on his face.

"You really need to get into better shape," he quipped as Harri finally got to his front stoop and instead of giving him a kiss on the cheek, she punched him in the arm.

"Ouch," he cried in mock pain. "And here I made you a nice cup of tea to welcome you home after a long day of work," he said and held up his FBI profiler mug filled with steaming green tea in front of her.

Harri smiled then and gave him a kiss. "You know me so well," she said. As she pulled away, she caught a whiff of mesquite smoke and smiled.

"Have you been making those ribs all day?" she asked.

Jake put his arm around her and gave her a big hug. "They came off the grill only a half hour ago. They've been waiting for you," he said.

Harri smiled and leaned into him as he closed the door behind her. She took the steaming mug of green tea out of his hand and he took her bag and jacket and put them on the chair next to his front door. Harri took a long deep sip of tea and let the warmth travel through her body.

"I so needed this," she said.

"I figured," Jake said. "When you didn't call me after your meeting with Addison James' mom I figured something was up."

Harri nodded, but she was more interested in his

phone calls to Interpol. Jake knew what she wanted. Grinning, he led her into the kitchen and with a flourish of his arm showed off his spread of corn on the cob, potato salad and delicious smelling baby back ribs.

"Wow. This looks beautiful and smells divine. I never knew what kind of an omnivore I was," she said.

"I am the grill master," Jake declared.

As Harri washed her hands in the sink, her mouth watered at the delicious food behind her. "What happened with the Interpol call?" she asked.

"Why don't we eat first," Jake said.

Harri could tell by the tone in his voice it wasn't going to be good news. She turned back to him and frowned as she dried her hands.

"They had no information on Jerome Wexler?" she asked.

"Even worse than that," Jake said.

Harri stepped back in surprise. "What could be worse than that?"

"They have no record of his private jet landing anywhere in the Netherlands on that date or any time after."

"What? How can that be?" Harri was shocked. "Oh, Jake. Honey I'm so sorry. I know what hell it was to get those flight manifests."

Jake nodded. "It was like a punch to the gut, I gotta be honest," he said.

Harri pursed her lips. Another dead end.

"Where does that leave us?" she asked.

"We stick with the plane," Jake said as he pulled a bottle of red wine from the rack. "The flight manifest was correct as far as the beginning part of the journey. We just need to track down where it really went. If we find some of the people who worked at the air strip back in '94, see if they might remember anything about the guy. The good thing going for us is he'd run for governor only a few years before that. He would be recognized."

"I'm sure if an employee at some rinkydink airstrip got to deal with the almost governor of Oregon, he might remember a conversation he had with him, even if it was twenty-five years later," she said.

"It's a stretch, I know, but it's all we have right now," he said as he polished off a rib.

Harri pulled plates and silverware out of the cupboards and handed one set to Jake. She loaded up her plate with potato salad and grabbed a buttered corn cob and three ribs. He did the same and they left the kitchen.

They sat next to each other at the dining room table, the lights of the LA basin twinkling behind them.

"What happened after your mother interview?" Jake asked.

"She couldn't give me much." Harri shook her head. "Levi Monroe had already given us all they both knew. Mom looks to have been a former actor or entertainer. She's maybe fifty and still stunning. Completely distraught over Addison's disappearance. Said the same thing Monroe did. Just couldn't believe she would ever run away and leave her guitar behind. Addison is an incredible guitar player. She was accepted to Julliard for early admission."

"That doesn't sound like she ran," he said.

"Right? I still haven't been able to talk to Jorge Hernandez. He was the lead detective on her disappearance three weeks ago. He's not returning my calls and I hope it's not because I stepped on his proverbial toes. He didn't do much investigating, though."

"Is that not like him?"

"No. It's not. He really is a good detective."

"What are you not telling me?" he asked.

"You haven't seen the news?" she asked.

Jake shook his head as he nibbled on a rib. "I was out enjoying the grilling and stayed off my phone."

"Sophie Lambert's body has been found. She was the girl Addison James was with when she disappeared. Best friends forever."

"Let me guess. Each of them told their parents they were sleeping at the other's house," he said.

"Ding. Ding. Ding. I don't know how parents even fall for that anymore," Harri said. "Anyway, I got a call from Detective Tom Bards."

"Really?" Jake asked.

"That was my reaction." Harri smiled. "Imagine my surprise. I have no idea how he convinced Richard Byrne to allow me to be anywhere near this case."

"Byrne probably didn't have a choice," Jake said.

"Anyway, Tom said the two cases were connected, which they are, and received formal approval for me to work under him and RHD."

"How long has Sophie been deceased?" Jake asked.

"Coroner thinks four days dead. She's expediting the autopsy. The parents want to make a positive ID tonight and there's still an unknown cause of death."

"How was she found?" he asked.

"People staying at the house. They found her in a wall," she replied.

Jake grimaced and put his rib down. "How in the world did she get into a wall?"

"That was my thought. She was wrapped in plastic, but not tightly enough. The remains leaked decomp fluids. The odor alerted the B&B guests who thought it was a dead rat."

"Shocking to find a body," he said.

Harri nodded and dug into her food. She didn't want to talk about decomposing bodies until, at least, after dinner.

They polished off the delicious meal in relative silence.

As they were cleaning up, Jake said, "You have another shot at RHD."

"Can you believe it?" Harri asked. "After what happened up in Oregon and that FBI prick calling everybody he knew, I thought I was toast. If it wasn't for Violet Howard, that might've been the end of me."

"No, Harri," Jake said. "You wouldn't be on this case if it wasn't for the Oregon case. Levi Monroe came to find you because of that case."

"I forgot to tell you." Harri turned to face him. "When I spoke to Addison's mother, she actually said she was the one that got Levi to come and find me. She followed the case on TV and when Addison went missing, she called Levi and told him about me."

"What'd I tell ya? A direct connection to the Oregon case," he said.

Harri nodded. Although she was happy to get another shot at getting into RHD, she wished it hadn't been from an outside source like Levi Monroe pulling strings to force Violet, and Gilead, and then Richard Byrne to give her the case. She would take it, though.

"You ready to hit the sack?" Jake asked with a twinkle in his eye.

"I think you can convince me of that," she said as the dimpled smile he gave her sent shivers up and down her spine.

For the millionth time, she wondered what Lauren would think about them together? Her little sister and her best friend getting together after all these years. Harri hoped she'd have a good laugh about it.

She followed Jake up the stairs.

Harri lay in bed listening to the coyotes howling outside. She checked her phone and saw that it was 3 a.m. This was typically the time the coyotes woke her up every single time she stayed at Jake's place. He never seemed to be affected by them and from the soft snoring coming from his side of the bed, tonight was no different.

Harri quietly slipped out of bed and padded across the room and down the stairs. She went down to the kitchen and poured herself a glass of water and grabbed the tub of ice cream she'd stashed there for just these nightly insomnia jags.

She sat down on the plush sofa and looked over the sleeping city. Where are you Addison? She sent her question into the night. And what did you two girls come face-to-face with? Her mind wandered over the last 48 hours' events and how different the life of girls who live in LA were compared to how she and her sister had lived in El Segundo.

El Segundo was part of the South Bay and was like a small, sleepy beach town. Very different than being in Hollywood. Where Addison James lived in Los Feliz was Hollywood adjacent. The surprising thing was that most of these girls tended to be very street smart because, after all, they grew up in a big city.

Something had made them comfortable enough to drop their guards. She thought of Sophie Lambert and her headshot. If Sophie had stumbled into some sort of opportunity as an actor, Harri could easily imagine

Addison going along to support her friend. It was definitely an angle to research because two girls who'd lived in LA all of their lives wouldn't so easily fall prey to the predators out there, even if they were only seventeen.

She opened the top of the ice cream and took out a big scoop. It was French Vanilla, her favorite. She sat and ate the ice cream and stared out into the city. Typically, she'd be up for hours until sun rose over the horizon and turned everything pink and orange. Not this time. She had a big day ahead of her and needed to get some sleep. She put the top back on the ice cream and took a big gulp of water. She'd have to try some of the breathing exercises from the app she'd put on her phone to get back to sleep. As she headed back upstairs to bed, she hoped she wouldn't dream of Addison James or Sophie Lambert.

9

DAY 2

The next morning, Harri and Detective Tom Bards met at the PAB and took an unmarked vehicle to Sophie Lambert's parents' house. The Lambert family lived in a sixteen-unit apartment building off of Commonwealth Avenue, also in Los Feliz.

Harri pulled the car in front of the hulking concrete building with little character and parked. As she got out of the car, she noted the raw gravel landscaping and trash scattered in places and thought this family was not doing as well as their neighbors.

It was an old building that wasn't kept up and Harri wondered how four people could live in a small apartment. She knew it happened all the time in Los Angeles due to incredibly high housing costs, but she couldn't imagine living with two kids in a small space like that. They had to get on each other's nerves.

Tom had gone over the case as it stood on their ride over. The parents had made a positive ID of their daughter Sophie Lambert the night before.

"The mother was pretty hysterical last night. We settled on this morning for an early meeting," he said.

Harri nodded. "Her grief must be unimaginable."

"It is."

Harri knew it was going to be a rough interview. They took the elevator up to the fourth floor and walked down the dark hallway to Unit 403.

Tom knocked on the door and it was opened immediately by a woman bearing a very striking resemblance to her daughter.

Elle Lambert had her black hair up in a messy bun. She wore a black maxi dress and her image was totally Hollywood cool. Her look, while current, was more for a twenty-something starlet and not a pushing fifties mom. But from the picture that Harri had studied earlier in the morning, Sophie was her mother's daughter.

"Please come in," Elle said.

She stepped back and Tom walked into the bright cheery living room, Harri right behind him.

Drew Lambert, a man who looked his age with thinning hair, stood up from the sofa and shook both of their hands.

Tom had told Harri that Elle was Sophie Lambert's full-time manager and the father was a freelance editor on numerous reality TV shows. He traveled a lot and wasn't home often, Tom had explained.

"Would either of you like a glass of water?" Elle asked. The puffiness in her eyes revealed she'd been crying all night.

"No, thank you," Harri said. "Is it okay if we record this interview?"

"Yes," Elle said as she glanced at her husband.

Drew nodded and Elle sat down next to him on the sofa.

Harri and Tom sat down in the club chairs across the coffee table from the Lamberts. Harri took out her phone and activated the recording feature.

"Tell us about that Friday," Tom began.

Elle looked at Drew and he gave her a nearly imperceptible nod. Harri guessed they'd spoken beforehand about who was going to fill in the narrative. Apparently, it had been decided Elle would do that herself.

"I last saw Sophie at breakfast," Elle began. "She had her usual, three hard-boiled eggs and coffee and then she went off to school."

"All right," Tom said. "What was the rest of her day like?"

"Well, she had an audition down on La Brea. It was for an independent feature," Elle added.

"They don't care what it was for," Drew said with a ragged voice.

"Well I'm sure they'll want to speak to the casting director of the film," Sophie said sharply.

Harri resisted the urge to look over at Tom but noted the apparent disagreement the parents were having.

"She said that audition went fantastic," Elle sniffed. "She was bubbly and happy. The casting director, Marguerite Wilson, had told her she would definitely be getting a callback."

"And she came back home after that?" Tom asked.

"She had to have, but I was unable to go with her because my other daughter, Andrea, had gotten into some trouble at school and I had to go have a parent-teacher conference. Otherwise, I always went with her to her auditions. I was at Andrea's school when she texted me saying she was on her way home. Then we ran errands, Andrea and me."

"Did you see her at all that day after she left for school?" Tom asked.

Elle dabbed at her eyes and shook her head. "I just got a couple more texts from her saying that she was going to Addison's house to sleep over. They did that all the time, so I didn't think it was a big deal."

"You said you found Addison James' cell phone in Sophie's room. When was that?" Tom asked.

"It was the next morning," Drew said. "I kept hearing a buzzing all night long. It was driving me crazy. I finally went into Sophie's room, even though she told me never to go in when she wasn't there. I found the phone under the bed."

"That's not like a teenage girl to leave her cell phone behind," Harri piped in.

"That's the thing," Elle looked at Harri. "The girls don't go anywhere without those phones. It's like they're attached to their hands. That was the first thing that got us worried. I called Addy's mom the moment Drew found the phone and that's when we figured out the girls weren't there. We called all her friends, but no one knew where they were. Or where they had gone off to." Elle's face became pale at the retelling of the story and her no-nonsense demeanor wilted.

"We're going to need a list of the names you called," Tom said.

"Also, who was your daughter's agent?" Harri asked.

"She has one of the best agents in town," Elle said proudly. "The Cosgrove Lucida Agency, CLA, on Rodeo in Beverly Hills. Derek Cosgrove is her agent. They said she would be the next Megan Fox."

Tears streamed down her face at what could have been. As Drew Lambert jotted down the names and phone numbers of the people they'd called looking for

Sophie, Tom nodded to Harri who took over the questioning.

"Do you know of anyone who might want to harm your daughter?" she asked.

"No," Elle said in surprise. "No, of course not. Everyone loved Sophie. She was a gorgeous girl who was the center of life at her school. She was kind to everyone and fun, and her career was starting to take off. She was always auditioning. Sophie was going to make it this year." With that, a sob escaped her lips.

Drew Lambert awkwardly patted his wife on the back as sobs overcame her and shook her body. He didn't look to be that affected, which Harri thought was interesting. Was he just numb? No, this was different.

Harri turned to Drew. "Mind if I use your bathroom?" she asked.

Drew nodded and waved toward the hallway.

Harri stood up and left the living room, peeking through the doors at the rooms beyond. She wanted to check out Sophie's room without any parents hovering around.

Harri first opened the door to what was obviously the master bedroom. She closed the door quietly and went to the next one. Harri opened the next door and saw a room that was painted in a lavender shade and was clearly shared by the two Lambert daughters. There were two single beds and one side looked more juvenile than the other. On what must be Sophie's side, there were photos of Sophie Lambert at all stages of growing up. She'd been a pageant baby all the way to a few years ago by the looks of the photos and awards.

Harri always found images of four- and five-year-olds in full makeup and big hair disturbing and that's exactly what she saw as she glanced at the pageant photos displayed on the shelves. Sky high shellacked hair with dark eyes and pink blush. So, her mother really had been grooming her to be part of show business for a long time.

Harri went over to Sophie's desk, but found it completely clean. No diaries or journals or anything. Kids kept all that stuff on their phones now. What they needed to do was get permission to go into her social media.

She left Sophie's bedroom and went to the bathroom and flushed the toilet to make it seem like she'd done her business. She walked back to the room and Elle had finally calmed herself down.

"Do we have your permission to get access to her social media?" Harri asked.

"Absolutely," Drew said immediately. "You can have her laptop if you want." He disappeared down the hallway where Harri had just been. He came back holding a bag with an Apple MacBook inside. "It should all be there," he said as he handed the bag to Harri.

"We're going to find who did this to your daughter," Harri said.

Tom gave her a sharp look but Harri ignored him. No police officer wanted to promise something that they couldn't deliver. Harri would do whatever was in her power to get Sophie justice.

Elle grabbed her hand and tearfully said, "Thank you."

Neither Harri nor Tom had anything further, so they stood up to go.

"We'll be in touch if we have any other questions," Tom said.

Drew nodded as Elle stood and sobbed into his shoulder again.

They left the couple as they were in their living room. As they turned toward the elevator bank, they saw a teenaged black-haired girl walking towards them, skateboard under her arm.

"Five dollars that's little sister," Harri whispered.

"Are you Andrea Lambert?" Tom asked.

"Who wants to know?" the girl responded warily.

"We're with the LAPD. Investigating your sister's death," he said.

The girl nodded.

"I'm Sophie's sister."

"When was the last time you saw her?" Harri asked.

Technically, they were supposed to get the parents' permission to speak to a minor, but they were in the hallway right outside the front door and Harri forged on.

"I saw her that Friday," Andrea said. "She was all excited. Going off to some Hollywood party with her friend. Addy."

Harri cleared her throat. "You have an address for this Hollywood party?" She asked.

"Sure, 'cuz I'm a limo driver," Andrea smirked.

"You got it, or not?" Tom snarled.

Andrea was defensive and Harri could guess why. She'd seen the bedroom she shared with Sophie. All the pictures and awards were of Sophie. None were of Andrea.

"I dunno. Something about the Hollywood Hills," she said. "That's all I heard when she was on the phone with Addy."

Tom raised his eyebrow at her.

"I was listening. So what?" she asked defensively.

"Did you hear anything else about the party?" Tom asked.

"No. That was it."

"Were you with your mom that day? She mentioned something about a parent-teacher conference?" Harri asked.

"That was earlier on that Friday. She dropped me off in front of the building after and then went to run some errands," he said.

Interesting, Harri thought.

Elle Lambert had said she'd been with Andrea running errands. It was a small omission, but one that might be useful later.

"Did you hear anything else about this Hollywood Hills party?" Tom prodded.

"No. That was it. I put my headphones on and played video games until she left. I feel bad now. I wish I'd said bye to her at least."

Tom nodded and let the girl by.

"If we need to ask any more questions, we'll talk to your parents. Okay?" Harri called after her.

"Sure, yeah whatever," she said and entered into the apartment.

Tom and Harri didn't speak until they were back in the car.

"Did you catch that lie that Elle Lambert told us?" Harri asked.

"About being with Andrea all afternoon? Yeah, I did. I don't think she was the one who stuffed Sophie Lambert into a wall, though. Looks like she thought Sophie was going to be her meal ticket," he said.

"Sophie had been a pageant girl from like the age of four. I think that mom really wanted her in show business," Harri said.

"Yeah, that was the feeling that I got, too. Mom probably was on the pageant circuit for a while back in her day. But a Hollywood Hills party. I bet you somebody at one her auditions knows something about that," Tom said.

"Then let's go to the agency next," Harri suggested.

"You drive. I'll find the address," Tom said.

Harri pulled out of the parking spot and headed south on Commonwealth toward Beverly Hills.

10

DAY 2

Debi Mills paced up and down the corridor, running through her lines. She had nearly killed herself getting to this car commercial audition on time even though she knew they'd be running late. She was right, of course, as it was three hours later, and she still hadn't been called in.

The casting office was in a nice location on paper, but her experience getting there threw her off her game completely. Finding a place to park was nearly impossible. When she finally found a spot on one of the side streets, she ended up across a major homeless tent city right off of Santa Monica Boulevard on Van Ness. She didn't scare easily, but she'd stepped on someone's belongings and two men had chased her down the road.

Frightened as all hell, she'd sprinted and completely messed up her carefully applied makeup. Not to mention she ended up being twenty minutes late.

She'd had to work the late shift at the diner the night before and hadn't learned her lines as well as she would have liked. After the first hour of sitting in the waiting room with all the other girls, she finally had to leave the room. She told the assistant she was right outside in the corridor running her lines.

That had been about an hour ago. She kept peeking her head in to see where they were at, but the assistant kept saying she was still a couple of people away. She focused back on the part she was preparing for.

Debi tried on the fake smile for her part as the kid in the back of the car. An actor playing her dad is speeding. Her line was 'Dad, you're driving too fast.'

The problem she had was the tone. She had said the line in a hundred different ways and she couldn't exactly get the point of the commercial. What was the message behind it? She didn't see the angle. She prided herself in always getting the angle of any commercial so she could get the right tone. This one was just not coming to her.

She bit her lip.

This was her fourth commercial with Nancy Grayson, the casting director that was in charge today. Nancy must like her because she kept calling Debi back in. August said that was a really good thing.

Her heart skipped a beat. She didn't want to mess up her good streak. She paced to the end of the corridor and came back again.

Why would a girl be in the back seat when her dad was driving his fast new Beemer? Why not the passenger seat? And why would a dad want to have his kid with him as he raced his new car? She sighed and tried the line again.

"Fancy seeing you here," a voice said from behind her.

Debi turned around and saw the woman named Georgie she'd met at her last audition. Debi gave her a big smile.

"This is a coincidence. Are you an actor?" Debi asked.

"Sometimes. My dad is Glenn Shipwell. You know that big western star from the seventies."

Of course, Debi had heard of him. Who hadn't? He was as popular as Clint Eastwood. He was a legend.

"Wow, you're his daughter?" she asked.

Georgie nodded. "Unfortunately. But I try not to think about that. So, I come and go into acting. I mean, I suppose it's what all kids of famous actors do. I actually do enjoy it, but I also don't love the way the industry kind of uses us up and throws us out. You know what I mean?" she asked.

Debi nodded.

She could only hope to be used at this point. She really needed to get her first job so she could get her SAG card. She hadn't been able to do that yet.

"How come you're out in the hallway?" Georgie asked.

"I'm running my lines. I know the line, but not my approach," Debi explained.

"Is Nancy running late again?" Georgie asked.

"You know Nancy Grayson, too?" Debi asked and then felt foolish. Of course, she would know all the casting directors in town. "That was a stupid question, never mind."

"I grew up here. You know how it is," Georgie said. "Speaking of acting, I have a fantastic coach I go to for lessons. He has a conservatory theater in Culver City. Have you heard of Desmond Ryan?" Georgie asked.

Debi's heart started beating faster. Everyone in town knew who Desmond Ryan was. He'd been in all the papers about how he was coaching the troubled star of the most recent Stars and Space flick. He was her acting coach, too?

"That's kind of amazing," Debi admitted.

Georgie cocked her head. "You want to come with me tomorrow?" she asked.

"Seriously, me?" Debi asked.

"Why not.? He loves having people audit his class. It's twenty-five dollars for four hours of magic. You will get so much out of it," Georgie said.

Twenty-five dollars was an amount she couldn't spare.

"I have to keep the afternoon open in case work calls. I'm on call," Georgie lied.

"I get it. Twenty-five bucks can be a lot for a beginning actor. Let me pick that up. I really want you to go. I can see how hard you work on your craft and you deserve to have the kind of education that Desmond provides."

Debi worked hard to keep her tears in. "Seriously, are you sure?" she asked.

"Absolutely," Georgie said. "My pleasure."

The door opened and the assistant poked her head out. "Debi Mills, it's your turn," she said.

Debi turned back to Georgie. "How do I contact you?"

Georgie pulled out her phone. "What's your number?"

Debi recited her number and Georgie texted back her contact info. Debi's phone pinged.

"Text me tomorrow morning. I'll send you the address," Georgie said.

Debi wanted to hug the woman, but she was a little shy. Instead, she waved good-bye and followed the assistant back into the room.

Desmond Ryan, Debi thought. How did I get so lucky? And Georgie, daughter of a famous actor, taking her to a famous acting coach's class. Debi felt like she was floating on clouds.

Her smile was a hundred watts when she walked into the audition and faced Nancy, the casting director, the producers, and two ad execs. Debi didn't bat an eyelash.

She was going to kill this audition.

11

DAY 2

Whatever Harri had assumed CLA Partners would be from speaking with Elle Lambert, she had been completely wrong. CLA Partners sat on one of the most impressive streets in all of Beverly Hills.

It was a gleaming white building five stories tall that overlooked Rodeo Drive. Harri was having a hard time connecting Sophie Lambert with such a place. Sophie was only seventeen and at the beginning of her career. This agency looked like it was for actors at the pinnacle of their careers.

She'd even heard of the agency even though she didn't follow the goings-on of Hollywood very much, though she had grown up in the area. It was in the periphery. Harri, consumed by her sister's disappearance, had never thought much of it.

When they walked to the lobby Harri turned to Tom. "Is that a Rothko behind the receptionist?" she asked.

Tom looked harder. "Bet you that it's real," he said in a singsong voice.

"With this address? Absolutely."

"Wasn't expecting this," Tom said.

"Neither was I," Harri said. "Sophie hadn't been in anything yet, had she?"

Harri assumed it would be difficult to find this kind of representation at the beginning of one's career. She was waiting for some megastar to walk right by them. Tom took out his police ID and showed it to the receptionist.

"We're here to meet with Derek Cosgrove. He's expecting us," he said in a clipped tone.

The receptionist nodded and looked at something on her computer screen. "He's on the fourth floor. You can't miss his office," she said as she pointed to a bank of glass elevators to the left. "Take those up," she said.

"Thank you," Harri said.

They left the receptionists and the brilliant red Rothko behind and stepped into the glass elevator. Tom punched in number four and the elevator silently rose up, giving them a fabulous view of Rodeo Drive.

"Fancy digs," Tom said.

"You sign with us, we will give you the world," Harri said.

"I wonder how true that actually is," Tom said.

"Same," Harri said.

The elevator dinged open and let them out into a large open-plan office. Harri looked past the small computer stations to a massive office beyond. Three desks stood near the door, young women with headsets all busy at their computers. Awards lined the walls behind them.

"This must be the office she was talking about," Harri said.

Tom walked over to the nearest assistant and cleared his throat.

The assistant looked up and frowned. "There's only supposed to be one of you," she said, looking pointedly at Harri.

"Mr. Cosgrove is expecting us. We're from the Los Angeles Police Department. This is Detective Harriet Harper and I'm Detective Tom Bards," he said, completely ignoring her rude remark.

The young woman flushed red and nodded. "One moment, please," she said.

She hurried out of her seat and knocked on the door. A muffled 'come in' came from inside and she peeked her head in.

"LAPD is here," she said.

She opened the door further and nodded at them. They were being led into the inner sanctum, Harri thought sourly. Who was this guy anyway?

They entered the large office and again were treated to an incredible view of Beverly Hills, West Los Angeles, and beyond that, the Pacific Ocean.

A man in his forties with a perfect salt-and-pepper crewcut and a hardbody jumped up from behind his desk and came over to them, pumping first Tom's hand and then Harri's.

"I'm destroyed by what happened to Sophie. I can't even get over it. She was on her way to being a star. No question," he said and directed them to a small seating area.

Cosgrove sat on the sofa, taking the entire space for himself. Harri and Tom seated themselves in the leather club chairs flanking both sides of the sofa. Harri was surprised he was going for the informal touch as he seemed like one of those power players that would get off on being behind a massive desk while talking to two lowly police detectives.

Derek Cosgrove didn't pull that power move. Instead, he sank low and deep into the soft leather sofa and looked at them expectantly.

"How can I help?" He placed his open hands on his knees, palms up. "You have to find out what happened to Sophie. It's such a tragedy. I'm destroyed," he added again.

"How long have you been representing Sophie Lambert?" Harri asked.

"About a year now," he replied. "She's been up for commercials and indie films. She was up for the love interest on one of the Alien Guard movies. Have you seen those?" he asked.

"No, I'm not that into superheroes," Harri said.

"She was on her way. The new Megan Fox. That blue-black hair and baby blue eyes and that face. Stunner. She had the look, just needed the first break to crack it open. And it was happening. It was happening."

"How did you come to discover her?" Tom asked.

"Uh, well. You must have met Elle Lambert already?" he asked.

"The parents made the identification last night," Tom said and let that sink in.

Derek Cosgrove blew out a breath. "That woman is the most ridiculous momager I have ever encountered."

"Momager?" Harri asked.

"Mom. Manager. A mother who needs her kid to be a star at any cost," Derek explained. "She'd been knocking on my door for years, trying to get Sophie representation since she was twelve. I don't rep kids. I waited until Sophie got a little older and picked her up when she turned sixteen. Once her looks had developed more."

Even though he had tried to say it diplomatically, it still came out ugly, Harri thought. A sixteen-year-old girl was nowhere near a woman and once again she was struck by how viciously commercialized the industry was to its young. Probably to everyone, Harri thought.

"We're trying to pinpoint all the people Sophie Lambert had contact with in the last three days before her disappearance. She disappeared on October 19. That was a Friday night," Harri began.

Derek Cosgrove held up a hand to stop her. "I made sure to have one of my assistants put a list together for you. We know she disappeared that Friday night and we'd hoped she'd turn up. We had so much lined up for her. As the weeks went by and then she never checked in, no one heard anything. I worried this might be the outcome, but I still held out hope."

"Did anyone come to speak to you after she disappeared?"

"No one contacted me," he said with a shrug.

Harri did what she could to hide her annoyance. This case hadn't been handled right from the beginning. What was wrong with Jorge Hernandez?

Derek pulled out his cell phone and dialed a number. "Taylor, bring in the Sophie Lambert paperwork," he said.

He hung up the phone without waiting for an answer and moments later a soft knock sounded at the door. The door opened and another young assistant came in with a manila envelope. She handed it to Derek who handed it to Harri. Irritation flashed through Harri at his assumption that she was the one who dealt with the paperwork.

Harri opened the manila folder and saw a sheet with a list of 13 auditions for the week before Sophie Lambert had disappeared along with addresses, the names of the production company, and the casting directors.

"Who would be the best person to speak to about getting a list of other actresses at each one of these auditions?" Harri asked.

"Talk to the casting directors first," Derek said. "They should have a list of everyone they called in, who showed up, and they could probably give you tape on all of them. If you want."

"What do you think happened to Sophie Lambert?" Tom asked.

"She met the wrong person," Derek said. He looked past them with a grim look on his face.

"Did you hear of any wild parties that week?" Harri asked.

"In this town? There's a party every night. Just depends what part of town and what your poison is," Derek said.

"Did Sophie Lambert participate in that kind of stuff?" Harri asked.

"I have no idea." Derek shrugged and sighed. "I imagine Elle Lambert would keep a tight leash on Sophie. She was her meal ticket, after all. I'd hope she'd have enough sense not to send a seventeen-year-old out to the party circuit."

"Would Elle think Sophie dating someone famous would help her career?" Harri asked.

"I see you understand how aspects of this town work," Derek said with a smile.

"Was she that hungry?" Tom asked.

"I don't know," Derek said with another shrug. "Elle had been dragging that kid all over town for years. If she wasn't in school or an audition, Elle had her in a class or networking group or some other shit. Elle was convinced that all it would take was for the right person to get a look at Sophie. And she was probably right. Look, there's talented actors and beautiful actresses. I'm not saying that actresses can't be talented, but you also gotta be beautiful. I mean you can't totally suck, and you can't be a raging bitch, either. Not at first. But what I'm saying is that it's the face or bod that opens the doors. At some point, yeah, you gotta know your craft and you'll either sink or swim with good and bad projects. That's my job. I don't put my people in stinkers. Otherwise, I wouldn't be able to afford such a humble office. I know a good project and I don't waste my people's time on anything else. Why bother? I don't know much about my actors' personal lives, but they have to be clean, punctual, and know their lines. I drop clients if they become a mess. That's a liability for everyone and a waste of time and money."

The room fell silent for a moment as Harri and Tom took in everything Derek Cosgrove had just said.

"So, you're saying you never knew Sophie to have any drug or alcohol problems?" Harri asked.

"From my side, absolutely not. She was punctual. She knew her lines and every casting director was happy with her audition. She was a great client and I'm telling you, that face was gonna break hearts all over this town before she even got on screen," he said.

"Thank you, Cosgrove," Tom said standing up.

Harri followed suit and Derek followed them to the door.

"Before you go, can I ask you to do something for me?" Derek asked.

They both turned back to him and Tom said, "Sure."

"Find the son-of-a-bitch who did this," Derek said. "Sophie didn't deserve that."

Harri could swear she saw a tear forming in his eyes. He was a good actor, she thought, then immediately felt bad for being so cynical. Maybe he actually cared about her. Or was it because he'd lost a valuable client with no return on his investment?

Harri and Tom returned to the building lobby and Tom gave the valet their ticket. They waited to speak until they were safely back in the cruiser.

As Harri turned right onto Rodeo, her thoughts went back to Sophie.

"Didn't sound like Sophie was a partier," Harri remarked.

"But would he even know that? It didn't seem like her mother would have minded if she'd been rubbing elbows with the Who's Who of LA," Tom said.

"Would a mother allow her teenage daughter to drink or do drugs? That wouldn't make her a star. You heard him. He'd drop her as a client."

"And why are you thinking that she was using?" Tom asked.

"There's no obvious cause of death. No obvious signs of violence on her body. I'm thinking we're going to find drugs," Harri said.

"This is when I feel fortunate to have grown up in a hayseed town. I would have hated to be brought up here," Tom said.

"I was brought up in Southern California. It wasn't all that bad. But then I did live in El Segundo and that was a world away from Hollywood," Harri said as she maneuvered the cruiser onto the 10 Freeway.

"Were you a little surfer girl, Harri?" Tom teased her. "A little beach bunny?"

He chortled to himself even after she shot him a look of death.

"I'm thinking we split up the casting directors to see how much we can get from them before this story hits all the papers," Harri said.

"You think press will stop people from talking to us?" Tom remarked.

"If there are drugs involved, they'll put the blame on the victim," she said.

"You're right about that," Tom said. "You gonna tell me what that was all about with the envelope?"

"Did you see him hand it to me like I was your secretary or something?"

"Oh, is that it?" Tom laughed. "I could tell you were annoyed, just wasn't sure why." Tom looked at the information from Derek Cosgrove. "We have a lot of people to interview."

"We could get lucky and find what we need on the first one," Harri said hopefully as she took a right onto Main Street.

She was glad to be back in the gritty world of downtown Los Angeles. It felt more real than the gleaming white tower they'd just been in.

She thought once again of the glittering facades that Hollywood offered the world. The building was literally an ivory tower, but the business preyed on the dreams and sometimes the flesh of the young hopefuls flocking into the industry, determined to see their name in lights. Harri pushed that thought to the back of her mind. She needed to focus on Addison and how she got mixed up in all of this.

DAY 2

J ake Tepesky walked into the Bradbury Building on South Broadway and once again marveled at the ironwork atrium. He'd been excited to see the Bradbury Building for the first time after seeing Blade Runner, the 1981 movie that had prominently featured the building.

The movie became a favorite of his and Lauren's. They'd visited every location from the film they could find when they were freshmen in high school. At one point, Jake had been so inspired by the building he even thought of becoming an architect, but then Lauren disappeared, and his life trajectory changed forever.

He watched the ornate elevator slowly rising to the third floor. The sight reminded him of one of the first images of this interior in the movie. The red brick building from the outside looked like any other old office building. If a person didn't know what it was, they would walk right by it. But if they walked inside and looked up, they'd see a glass ceiling and some of the most ornate ironwork on the West Coast circulating around the light-filled space, with glass elevators rising up and down between the balconies.

However much he loved the building, there was no way Jake was getting into that elevator. First, they were the original elevators from 1893. Second, he was claustrophobic in elevators already.

The FBI offices were on the third floor and he took the stairs two at a time. He was an old hat at stairs seeing as he lived on top of a steep hill. He smiled at the memory of Harri swearing up a blue storm the second time she came to his home. She still gasped at the top of the stairs. He took it as his exercise for the day.

When he got to the third floor, he looked into the camera and the door buzzed open. Special Agent Leonora Dean in Cybercrime was expecting him. He went to the front desk, showed his credentials, and signed in. Leonora turned up behind the receptionist and smiled.

"Jake Tepesky! It's been too long," she said.

"It has been," Jake said as he turned to face the tall, slim, brunette.

"Do you miss us at the FBI at all?" Leonora asked.

Jake shrugged and then nodded and then shook his head no.

"At least you're honest," she said.

It had been six years since Jake walked away from his career as an FBI profiler. He'd traveled all across the country profiling on open cases of rapists, murderers, and terrorists. Then one day he found himself in a hotel room, unsure of the city he was in, and another file to work on and he decided to come home.

Now he was a consultant for private businesses and police departments. He helped them screen potential clients and employees. It was boring work, but it paid well. The difference was that he was back in control and could say no if he wanted to or needed to. He also didn't need to see what human monsters did to their prey.

Jake frowned at that thought. He'd been seeing bodies for the last four months. First, it was the Creek Killer and then the bodies up in Oregon.

But he'd found Lauren, like he'd sworn he would all those years ago. He knew becoming an FBI profiler had helped find her, but that had been more about Harri, her little sister. Little sister with whom he was now in a relationship.

"You still with me, buddy?" Leonora asked.

"Sorry. It's been a while since I've been in an FBI office," he said.

"I heard you had quite the run-in with an agent up in Oregon," she said.

"Wow. Forgot how fast the FBI gossip train travels," Jake said.

"I know that guy. He's a dick," Leonora said.

"Better be careful what you say, Leo. Somebody connected might hear you," Jake remarked.

Leonora rolled her eyes and waved him off. "Follow me," she said.

"How's Danny?" Jake asked as he followed down a hallway.

Daniel Dean was Leanora's husband, a professor of Anthropology at UCLA and lover of Pinot Noir. Jake had a momentary pang of guilt about not getting together with them when Leonora first transferred to this field office.

Jake hadn't been ready to make contact with any of his FBI pals because of his own last case. It had stayed with him worse than any other and was the reason he finally walked away from the agency.

"He's doing great. He loves UCLA. We really should get you out to dinner, or for some Pinot," she said.

"I was just thinking the same thing," he said.

"Here it is," she said with a flourish of her arms as if she was on a game show and presenting the amazing prizes. "The LA outpost of the Violent Crimes against Children Program."

Jake took a slow glance around the room and noted the bank of cubicles with agents scrolling through social media accounts, chat rooms, and computer code. Each station had multiple monitors and there were more agents across from them in what looked like listening booths. They wore gaming headsets and all of them were chatting away with some child predator.

Jake pushed the thought away. "It's all online now, isn't it?" he asked.

"Almost exclusively," Leonora confirmed. "Some of it's still done old-school, but online is the richest hunting ground for them."

Leonora noticed Jake looking at the agents in the booths. "They're using voice-changing software," she said. "Makes them sound young, or feminine, whatever spider they need to be to catch the fly."

"Let's go into my office and you can tell me more about this guy you're looking for," she said.

Jake nodded and watched as an agent typed a bunch of heart emojis into a chat box as he passed her station.

"This is such soul-sucking work," he observed.

"It sure is but every single time one of them goes down, I can sleep a little better at night," Leonora said.

Jake sat down across from her in her small, tidy office.

"I'm surprised posing like kids still works. You'd

think they'd change their methods after seeing a few of their friends busted on TV," Jake said.

"No, that's what you would do because you're smart and also not a criminal," Leonora said as she sat at her desk. "I don't want to say pedophiles are stupid, but they have their urges and my agents really can come off as a ten-year-old boy or a twelve-year-old girl. Sometimes even younger."

A shiver ran down Jake's spine. An image of the graves from Oregon popped into his head and once again, he pushed it away.

"You ever heard of Jerome Wexler?" he asked.

Leonora shook her head no. "You mentioned his name on the phone and I did a little digging to see what he was about," she said.

"You were always the best at research. Did you find anything after 1994?"

"Nope. Nothing. He escaped on that private jet and was never heard from again apparently," she said. "When the police looked into him at the time there were all the usual flags put out to the agency and we alerted Interpol, but there was never a hit."

"He stole money from his primary client. A multi-millionaire who made his fortune in hardware stores. The old guy had a lot of cash. Wexler set up this camp through a few shell corporations and used the site as a child pornography movie studio, as well as a private pedophile resort of sorts. He could have absconded with up to three hundred million."

Leonora grimaced. "I read the reports from your time in Oregon," she said.

Jake's eyebrows raised. "Really? How'd you get your hands on those?"

"The CEHTTF has jurisdiction on those types of

crimes. My division is international, actually. But we play nice and share our things."

"The FBI loves their letters, don't they," Jake said.

"We do," Leonora smiled and nodded her head. "The Child Exploitation and Human Trafficking Task Force is what that stands for. In any case, I was able to get the FBI file on Black Rock Island. Jerome Wexler is not mentioned anywhere."

"Is that so?" Jake was surprised.

"Yes, the name on the top was Chris Becker, who, from what I understand, was the son of some millionaire up there. Supposedly, he was the mastermind of the operation."

"Impossible." Jake shook his head. "Chris Becker was a victim of the camp. He was just a kid when it was active."

"That makes sense," she said. "You've gotten a lot further than they have. They're still looking into the shell corporations set up for that camp on the island."

"That's disappointing I honestly don't know what else to say on that. I don't understand why they would be dragging their feet, or throwing Chris Becker under a bus," Jake said.

"Well," Leonora shrugged. "Dead men tell no tales, and they make for great fall guys because of it."

She let that hang in the air for a moment and Jake took it all in.

"Okay, well I wanted to come see you today because of Jerome Wexler," he said. "We know once a pedophile always a pedophile. He's definitely out of the country and so far, I've found no trace of the private jet, the money, or him."

"I'm listening," Leonora said, sitting back in her chair.

"Have your teams uncovered trafficking or child pornography rings with large funding sources? I'm talking wealthy men with access to kids. That seems to be the kind of people Wexler catered to."

"We've found Asian conglomerates that deal heavily in the sex slavery trade, but the one that we've been looking at recently is out of Europe, specifically Russia. That crew seems to be swimming in money. Have you seen the stories about the women from Eastern Europe with the barcodes on their necks or arms? That's their mark of property. We haven't been able to get close to the power center yet because it's in Moscow."

"I wouldn't be surprised if the Russian officials have their fingers in that pie," Jake said dryly.

Leonora nodded. "If this guy only likes the uber rich, I can imagine him having some interaction with this organization. They traffic in all ages, male and female. They're latest move is preying on Syrian children coming over the borders unaccompanied."

"Spoils of war," Jake said bitterly.

"Did you ever clue on any viable aliases for Wexler?" she asked.

"No, and believe me, I've looked."

"He had to have had at least one new identity well-established before he got on that plane."

"That's my assumption, as well."

"You've given us a lead with the plane information," she said.

"I'm trying to uncover where it landed back in 1994. I spoke with Interpol in the Netherlands and they have no record of the plane or Wexler ever entering the country."

"Ah, that's why you're really here. You want me to track down this jet?" she asked.

"I don't have access to your databases anymore," he reminded her.

"I'll see what I can find," she said.

Jake smiled. "Thank you. Any new groups I uncover, you'll be the first to know," he said.

"I should hope so, Jake," she said. "How are you feeling after finding Lauren Harper finally?"

Jake's heart dropped. He wasn't sure how he felt about finding Lauren. He was happy he finally had a place to go and talk to her. He hoped she was at peace. Neither he nor Harri were any closer to uncovering who had killed her. The frustration of that kept him up at night.

"She was alive for a year before they killed her. That information has been hard to deal with. We need to find him," he said.

Leonora nodded and didn't say anything. She didn't need to. They sat quietly for several moments, thinking of the implications of the case.

Jake cleared his throat. "Thank you so much for meeting with me on such short notice. You've given me hope," he said and stood up to go.

"Jake, if he's still out there, we'll find him," Leonora promised. She pulled herself up from her seat and came around her desk. She wrapped him in a big hug.

"We have to do dinner this month," she said. "Danny and I won't take no for an answer. And don't tell me your busy. Everyone's busy. We want to meet Harri and Danny has a new Pinot he's saving for a special occasion."

Jake nodded and promised they would.

She led him out of the office and he kept his composure until he heard the click of the door behind him. He walked quickly down the hall, away from the prying eyes of the FBI camera.

He clutched the iron banister and took deep breaths. His anxiety rushed through his body and his fingers and toes tingled with the adrenaline.

Jake breathed in.

One, two, three.

Breathe out.

His breathing technique took about ten minutes to calm him down enough to walk. He swayed a little on his feet, but he was okay enough to drive. The walk to the parking structure would expel some more adrenaline as well.

13

DAY 2

Detectives Harri Harper and Tom Bards walked into Exam Room One at the Los Angeles County Medical Examiner – Coroner's Office for the autopsy of Sophie Lambert.

Their plans to separate and speak to the casting directors had been dashed when the coroner's office called and the assistant asked if they could make it to the coroner's office right away. It had taken them only twenty minutes to get there.

Dr. Leanne Grimley nodded to them and turned to her assistant. "Detective Harriet Harper and Detective Tom Bards have entered Exam Room One to observe the autopsy of Sophie Lambert, age seventeen," she said.

The coroner was in full medical gear, all her instruments placed on a tray next to her. Harri and Tom had both put on paper medical robes on top of their clothes and paper booties over their shoes to make sure they didn't bring any of the outside world onto Sophie Lambert's body. When Harri first saw Tom with the paper cap on, she wanted to laugh but held it in. She knew she looked just as ridiculous.

Dr. Leanne Grimley removed the sheet from Sophie Lambert and Harri forced down the wince that came whenever she saw a dead body. Sophie had been a beautiful girl. Now, her skin was mottled and disfigured. Decomposition was far along and the smell was overwhelming. The body was disfigured with gas and when Dr. Grimly made the chest incision, the gas came out in a swoosh. Harri stepped back.

"She's definitely in a later stage of decomp," Dr. Grimley said.

She took each one of Sophie's organs out, weighed them, documenting color and appearance. The doctor checked all the different cavities and documented the various cuts, contusions, and damage.

Harri couldn't help but tune out some of the damage done to this poor girl's body. She had evidently been raped multiple times and it was hard for Harri to keep listening.

According to the coroner, Sophie had no signs of ligature marks on her wrists and ankles. She had been kept somewhere, so that likely meant drugs. How else would they have controlled her? She was also starved, apparently. Her recent weight loss was a sign of that, as well as the fact the cuticles on her fingernails had receded.

"The heart has signs of acute myocardial infarction," Dr. Grimley said.

"Heart attack?" Tom asked.

"Appears so," Dr. Grimley said.

"She was only seventeen," Tom said.

"I've sent hair samples to the lab as well as all samples from under her nails. Hopefully that will give you some information about where she's been and who she's been with. The toxicology report is back. I sent it out yesterday. They found Fentanyl and Heroin in her system," she said.

"Are you thinking overdose?" Harri asked.

"She didn't have enough in her system to OD. She might have had an unknown underlying heart condition. When you're seventeen, you believe you're invincible. If her heart hadn't caused her any trouble how would she know?" Dr. Grimes asked.

"Are you marking this a suspicious death?" Harri asked.

"I need more time with the heart," Dr. Grimley said. "As of right now, I'll be ruling her death as a heart attack, results pending. I've swabbed her orifices for semen. I'll let you know those results when I get them."

Harri and Tom exchanged a look. Could Sophie's death have simply been a terrible accident? The body was dumped in the house to hide the fact she'd been held and raped repeatedly. It was possible that wasn't the desired end point. Addison could very well still be alive. Drugged up, but alive.

The two detectives stayed for the rest of the autopsy, but Dr. Grimley didn't have any more revelations for them. They got her permission to leave and she granted it.

"You were right," Tom said.

"About the drugs? Yeah, ten points for me," Harri said rolling her eyes as they made their way out to the cruiser. "I'm wondering if this was an accidental death. The house was a body dump. But, why not leave her on the street to be found if it was accidental?"

"Yeah, the body in the wall was so dramatic," Tom agreed. "Maybe whoever dumped the body didn't know it was accidental. If she was being trafficked, then whoever dumped her might've thought one of the johns killed her."

"They had to know how strong the drugs they gave her were," Harri said as they approached the car.

"She didn't have enough in her system to warrant an overdose, though," Tom reminded her.

"Right, but Tom this means Addison could still be alive," Harri said.

"We should assume she is, but for how long is another question entirely."

"You think they'll try to get rid of her?" Harri asked.

"I would. Most likely sell her off to some group out of state. That means the clock just moved up, Harri. We're really running out of time here."

"Let's go work that list then. Find out about where the party was. This is clearly an organized operation."

"It could be a single person who took them," Tom said.

"Not two teenage girls, too much trouble. This had to be an organized effort."

"Harri, so far there's no real evidence of that. We can't just present one of your hunches without evidence," Tom said.

"Then let's go get it," Harri said.

14

DAY 2

Debi Mills pinched herself to make sure she wasn't dreaming. She'd just watched the most amazing performance she'd ever seen of a one-act play by two actors she'd seen in TV shows. Now, Desmond Ryan, the famous acting coach, went through the scene line by line, beat by beat, to show the actors how to better connect with each other and project emotion. Debi snuck a peek at Georgie.

Georgie smiled back at her. "Isn't this great?" she whispered.

"I can't believe I'm here," Debi said.

Desmond finished up giving kudos and critique to the two actors. The class erupted in applause. The two actors took a bow and went back to their seats.

Desmond handed out the assignments for the next class. Debi's chest constricted. What must it be like to be in the class, surrounded by the kind of actors she could dream of becoming, and doing this kind of work?

"Do you want to meet him?" Georgie asked.

Shyness suddenly came over Debi. "I'm sure he's so

busy. I wouldn't want to disturb him," she said, her heart pounding. Of course, she wanted to meet him, but she didn't want to come off as desperate.

Debi wished she had enough money to take classes like this. She'd absolutely book jobs within a month of lessons with Desmond Ryan. Adrenaline shot through her. Hearing the nuggets of technique made Debi crave more. Maybe she could audit more classes. Would he allow that? The cost of daily lessons would be impossible. But maybe she could do once or twice a week? Her mind raced with wondering how she could scrounge up twenty-five dollars for another class.

Acting was a constant communication between the people in a scene in the present moment, both in body movement and dialogue. On-camera work differed because the actor interacted with the camera almost as much as with another actor. Sometimes actors stood behind the camera to help keep that human connection, but not always.

The Desmond Ryan studio was nondescript and small. Someone of Desmond's stature could have a large open space with more students than were present at today's class.

Instead, the studio was tucked into a strip mall off National Boulevard in the Palms section of Los Angeles, an area she didn't know very well. Palms was just south of the 10 freeway and east of the 405 freeway. She'd ventured there only once before and had gotten lost looking for the address Georgie gave her.

Georgie interrupted her thoughts with a nudge. "I know you want to meet him," she said.

"I'm nobody, though and these actors are so talented," Debi said.

"He would love to meet you," Georgie said and pulled Debi up to her feet.

"I don't think I'm ready for this," Debi said, but Georgie ignored her.

They walked down the steps to where Desmond was talking to one of the male students. When he saw Georgie, a huge smile crossed his face.

"Georgie girl! So good to see you," he said and gave Georgie a bear hug. Then he turned his sharp brown eyes to Debi.

"Georgie mentioned you'd be auditing my class today," he said.

"Thank you so much for allowing me to experience this. It was amazing watching you work," Debi said.

"We had a full day of truth today." He nodded. "Angie and Martin really pushed themselves past their comfort boundaries and got down to the core of the scene. I love classes like this. It energizes me."

"Me too," Debi said. "I can barely stand still."

"I told you Desmond was the best," Georgie said with a wink.

"Well yes, I am. Thank you for saying so," Desmond said with a huge grin and a slight bow. A student behind him giggled.

"So, Des. Are you still doing private on-camera lessons?" Georgie asked.

"I am. You getting back into the game?" he asked.

"I'm always up for the game," Georgie said. "But I'm asking for Debi."

"Um, I don't, um, I'd love to but," Debi fumbled in a panic. She couldn't imagine what this man cost per hour.

Georgie put a hand on Debi's shoulder. She understood and stopped talking.

"If you're available, I'll contact you to set something up for Debi then," Georgie said.

Desmond nodded. "You know how to reach me. Excuse me, I need to talk to Kevin before he leaves."

He stepped away from them and Debi turned to Georgie.

"George, I can't pay for any of this," Debi whispered. Her cheeks burned and she could feel sweat gathering above her lip. If she could disappear from embarrassment, she would. "I haven't even booked my first job yet."

"That doesn't matter," Georgie explained. "If you spend time working with him, you will book."

Debi couldn't believe Georgie was going to make her say it again.

"Georgie, I can't pay for this. I can't even pay to audit the class. How in the world can I pay hundreds of dollars an hour for this teacher?"

"Darling, calm down," Georgie whispered back. "I'm paying for it."

Debi's eyes widened. "What are you talking about? Why would you pay for me to take classes? You don't even know me."

Georgie tucked her arm under Debi's and walked her out of the building. A gentle breeze cooled Debi's burning cheeks. The sky glowed in the purple and pink of a Los Angeles dusk.

"Look, Debi," Georgie began. "I have a ton of money. I've always had money, but it doesn't mean anything unless I use it. If I don't use my money to help others and uplift them, then it doesn't flow. Understand? Money is energy and it has to move. If I want more abundance, I have to give abundance. You're talented and I want to help you. I want to help your energy flow, too."

"But you've never seen me act," Debi countered.

"I had a good feeling about you when we first met," Georgie explained. "Then we met again, and I knew it was synchronicity. So, I asked Marguerite and Nancy about you. They both said you've got it."

"Why didn't I book those commercials then?" Debi asked. She wasn't born yesterday, and Georgie sounded too good to be true.

"I like mentoring younger actors. It's my give back. I know I was born into enormous privilege being my father's daughter. For years, I flitted around Hollywood, squandering my energy. Then I was exhausted. I had money and connections and privilege, but what good was it? That's when I learned about how energy works, and I had to decide what my value add would be. I've been around talented, devoted young actors my entire life and when I see honest people like you putting in the hard work, I want to help. Is that so horrible of me?" she asked.

"No," Debi said as she tried to focus her emotion. She really wanted to believe this was for real. Like really, really wanted to believe that such an opportunity could fall into her lap like this.

"Listen," Georgie said. "You have to do what feels right for you. If you don't want private lessons, you don't have to have them. Okay?"

"Okay," Debi said. She wanted those damn private lessons, though.

"Why don't you come to a party with me tonight?"

"I'd love to come with you to a party but," Debi said thinking of the extra shift she'd signed up for that night.

"Hollywood works on connections," Georgie said.

"You have the talent, so you're way ahead in the game there. What you need is to be seen at the right parties by the right people. I'm sure you know this already since you didn't get to town yesterday."

"I do know that," Debi confessed.

"Think about whether it's right for you to start working with Desmond. Until then, you come with me tonight and meet some of my friends," she said.

Debi nodded, her mind buzzing. Connections were everything in Hollywood. Friends hired friends. Georgie seemed to be everyone's friend and that made Debi feel special. She deserved some good luck in her life, didn't she?

"What time is the party tonight?" she asked. She needed to call Junior to fill her shift tonight. She'd never switched shifts before with anyone and hoped that he'd forgive her on the short notice.

"Send me the address and I'll be there," Debi said.

"I'll come pick you up. Text me your address. Wear something sparkly," Georgie said and with a little wave, she got into the white BMW parked in a handicap spot.

"You need a ride?" she asked.

Debi shook her head no and watched Georgie drive off. She wasn't sure exactly what had just happened. Whatever it was, she decided to embrace it. Georgie was right. She needed flow in her life. If she kept doing what she was doing, she would only continue getting what she'd gotten. Things didn't change for her until she left home. Maybe it was finally time for that next step.

Debi let out her breath. Georgie wanted to take her by the hand and lead her into something bigger. Like straight into an honest-to-goodness Hollywood party. Debi walked to her car as she sorted through her wardrobe in her mind for something sparkly.

15

DAY 2

Detective Harri Harper gripped the steering wheel tightly as she pulled away from the third casting office on their list. Detective Tom Bards sat in the passenger seat reading through the list of actors they'd received at Nancy Gray's office. She'd driven them the entire day and was glad for that. She could pay attention to the road and not to her thoughts.

They'd struck out at the first three casting offices so far. Marguerite Wilson, Nancy Grace, and Rose Allen had no insight or information to give the detectives about Sophie Lambert.

Harri wasn't sure exactly what she expected them to tell her, but she hadn't thought they'd get a big fat zero. Harri hoped someone, one of the coordinators or assistants, might have seen Sophie talking to someone. Any information the detectives could use to narrow down the immense number of names they'd received. Unfortunately, all they received were even more people who needed to be interviewed. Harri and Tom would need to cold call close to two hundred women. They were going to need help with that.

"Explain to me again how this whole casting process works?" Tom asked. "How did three casting directors see so many girls in those couple days?"

Harri had spoken to one of the casting directors; assistants to get an overview. The assistant's explanation helped her get a handle on the world Sophie Lambert was navigating before she disappeared.

"Well, this is how that woman explained it to me," Harri began, hoping she was getting it right. "The marketing team at a company hires an ad agency to create a campaign. These ad agencies have a team of consultants they hire consistently to make the commercials and that includes directors, who hire the writers and crew, and then the casting directors. They decide the type they're looking for and the casting directors have these rosters for each look."

"Look?" Tom asked.

"Like girl-next-door, sexy siren, suburban mom, edgy millennial..."

"I get it." Tom nodded. "What's my look?"

Harri glanced at him. "Disgruntled cop?"

"No," Tom shot back. "I'm handsome, driven detective."

"Cool," Harri smiled. "I stand corrected. So, from what the assistant told me, this way of working is different than the way films and TV shows work."

"Different how?"

"To book a job, or getting according to the lingo, requires a look and not necessarily any acting talent."

"So, these girls should all have the same look as Sophie Lambert?"

"Affirmative."

"Did this assistant say what Sophie Lambert's look was?"

"Hot girl," Harri said with a grimace.

Tom didn't have a response to that. He just looked pointedly at Harri and then shook his head.

Harri Harper pulled up to an office building in North Hollywood. The neighborhood was still in a process of gentrification and while some people wanted to say it was coming up as a place for artists and creatives, Harri recognized it for what it was – an area struggling to shed its violent and impoverished past.

"Is it just me, or does this place look a bit less money?" Tom remarked.

"Hopefully, these people interacted more with Sophie than the other casting directors," Harri said.

"Here's hoping," Tom said.

"The other places were more established, running like machines. A small startup like this would need to work differently, stay nimble to be competitive."

"I hope you're right," Tom said. "We gotta find a way to trim this list."

Harri stepped out of the car, bag in hand. Tom checked his phone as he got out and followed Harri into the building.

"It's on the ground floor," he said and pointed to the first door to the left.

They walked across the lobby and into the offices of Helena McCarthy Casting. They found themselves in a tiny reception area with two plastic chairs. A receptionist sat in front of a computer to the left of an interior door.

This agency was decidedly more down-rent than the

Marguerite Wilson or Nancy Gray Agency. Harri approached the receptionist and flashed her badge.

"We have an appointment with Helena McCarthy," she said. "I'm Detective Harri Harper and this is Detective Tom Bards."

The woman nodded and before she could do anything else, a slim woman with a blonde ponytail came out of the back office. She shook both Harri's and Tom's hands with a smile.

"It's a pleasure to meet you," she said. "I'm Helena McCarthy. Please come in."

She led them to another tiny office, every surface piled high with head shots.

"I printed out the names of the actresses I saw that week like you requested," Helena said. She sat down behind her desk and Harri perched on another plastic chair as Tom leaned against the door.

"How else can I help you?" she asked.

"We need to track anyone Sophie Lambert crossed paths with in the days preceding her disappearance," Harri said. "Did you hear of any Hollywood parties that Friday night?"

Helena sighed and then smiled ruefully. "There are parties every night all over town. I didn't hear of anything, but then I wouldn't. I'm out of that loop. I don't go out because I no longer have to." She smiled again and then reached for a folder on her desk. "I have the list of actors who auditioned on the same day Sophie did. The job was an Internet-only commercial for an insurance company and Sophie, from what I remember, did a really good job."

Helena handed them glossy printouts of dozens of women who looked almost exactly like Sophie Lambert.

Dark hair, bangs, and light eyes. It was a look that styled a vintage pinup look.

"These women all look alike," Harri remarked.

"That's kind of how the commercial game works," Helena said. "The ad agency gives us the type they're looking for and we find it for them. This brief says that they were looking for a sultry sexpot with dark hair and light eyes. So that's who we called in," she said.

Harri handed the glossy printout to Tom who looked through the doppelgänger photos and shook his head.

"It's incredible there'd be close to thirty women who looked exactly like her," he said, waving the photo around.

"It's the small-town to Hollywood chain," Helena explained. "They were all the prettiest girl in their hometown. The prom queen. Everyone tells them they're beautiful enough to be on screen, so they all come here and find out there's literally dozens of others in town who look exactly like them."

Helena was a striking woman herself and Harri wondered if she'd been an actor. What small town had she escaped from?

"You mind my asking how long you've been operating?" Harri asked.

"Not at all," Helena said. "I used to be in the game. I had years where I made six figures as a commercial actor, but I knew it was just a matter of time before I aged out. An opportunity presented itself for some casting work and I took it. I didn't realize at first how good I would be at it, or how much I would enjoy it. I worked on my credits until I opened my own agency seven years ago. We've only been in this location three years. I was operating out of the back of my house before then.

"Can you tell us more about Sophie at the audition?" Harri asked.

"I looked over my notes from the day." Helena pointed to the folder she'd given Harri. "She'd nailed the audition, but we didn't go with her due to her height. The male actor was too tall, and the producers wanted a better match for him. Sophie was my second choice, as you'll see in the notes. If anything fell out with him, I would have resubmitted her."

"Did Sophie know that was why she didn't get the part?" Harri asked.

"Oh, no," Helena said. "We didn't notify. It's in the notes."

"That's a tough break. Not getting the job because of your height," Tom said.

"It is, but you have to be careful," Helena said. "If you tell them, some people understand it's just not meant to be, but others...don't do as well with rejection. Helena bit her lip as if she wanted to say something else.

"What are you not telling us, Helena?" Harri asked.

"I'm not really sure how to say this," she hesitated.

"You can't shock us," Tom said.

"Okay, well," Helena smoothed her already smooth ponytail. "There have always been rumors about young girls and powerful men around town. This is more than random to me, two incidents. It's just you asked about parties and a young girl is dead..."

Harri leaned in closer. She knew how to listen when a witness spoke, to give them space to continue their story. People hated a gap in conversation and tried to fill it and Harri really wanted this woman to talk.

"I don't know the whole story and so I don't want to give it to you secondhand," Helena continued nervously.

"I mean it's a story as old as Hollywood, but lately these rumors just sound different."

"Different how?" Harri asked.

After a pause, Helena closed her eyes and continued. "Familiar. There's something about these latest rumors that feel similar to rumors I was hearing right before something terrible happened to someone I used to know."

"What terrible thing happened, Helena?" Tom asked softly.

"A woman I used to know was assaulted at a party by someone high-up the Hollywood food chain. Someone big. I was at the tail end of my acting career and would see her, for coffee and around you know. She disappeared for a while and then the few times I saw her after she wasn't the same person."

"Did she go to the police?"

"No." Helena shook her head, speaking only to Harri. "She'd already been through too much. You know how it is. But she'll talk to you, I think."

"What's her name?" Harri asked.

"Roxanne. Roxanne Miles. I don't have her address, but I have her number." Harri wrote down in her notebook the information Helena showed her from her own phone.

"Did she get in trouble with drugs?" Tom asked.

"I don't know the details," Helena said. "She's really the best person to talk to about that. I honestly feel like I'm betraying her even mentioning her name because she was absolutely terrified when I spoke to her last. I just, I don't know…" Helena drifted off and stared out her window to the parking lot.

Harri couldn't read the woman. "Thank you for

having the courage to give us this information," Harri said.

Helena nodded. "You know, acting is hard enough. It takes a lot of emotional work. But it's the business that's so horrible on a woman. We're judged on our looks constantly and it gets into our psyche, you know? But that's the job. The extra stuff that happens to women in this town should be illegal. I know the #metoo movement is bringing these stories to light. But there are just so many stories."

Harri gave Tom a sideways glance. He nodded slightly in return. The interview was over. They wouldn't get any more out of Helena. She'd given them a lead. A name. They said their goodbyes and left the office.

" You wanna take Roxanne?" Tom asked when they got back into the car.

"You don't want to go together?" Harri asked.

Tom kept his eyes on the agency door, deep in thought.

"She'll have an easier time telling her story if I'm not there," he said.

"I think you're right," Harri said. "You'll start on the list of actresses?"

"I'll start the calls tomorrow," Tom said. "I have a hunch I'll find more drugged and assaulted actresses in our files. This seems like a smooth operation. If they've been operating for a while there are more victims out there."

"Wouldn't we have heard about them?" Harri asked as she got back onto the freeway and headed back to the PAB.

"Well, if the victims even came forward. If their claims were believed. If the investigations weren't swept under the rug, then yeah, we might have heard something about it, but I want to dig up partial cases like this. How much information is sitting in dead files of cases that went nowhere?"

They didn't talk much as she drove back downtown. She was thankful for the silence.

Harri couldn't shake her sadness at hearing of how Sophie lost a job because she was too short. If she wasn't a good match for the actor, if she didn't meet the requirements of the job, why did they make her audition? Did she come out of the audition thinking she hadn't done a good enough job? That she wasn't attractive enough?

The casting directors, the directors, and the producers held so much power over these girls. Power they could wield at any moment to get what they wanted. No one had even mentioned if Sophie was talented or not. She was just too short. Harri shivered involuntarily.

"You all right?" Tom asked.

"Feel like I'm gonna have nightmares after today," Harri said.

"Why?"

"The brutality inflicted on these female psyches," Harri said. "They come here with a big dream and work so hard and then it's like, you're too short. Next."

Tom smiled. "Okay, Harri. You ever been to basketball tryouts?"

Harri shot him a look.

"They want to act, though. The girls choose this profession," Tom reminded her.

"Did Sophie, though?" Harri argued. "Elle Lambert had her in pageants since she was in diapers. She was trying to get her an agent since she was twelve. Was it Sophie's dream, or Elle's? I mean what does a twelve-year-old girl know? And why wouldn't a mother protect her daughter from this?"

"If the girls make it, they have fame and fortune."

"How many make it, though? And if they do, what kind of damage are they carrying around?"

"Probably not as much as a kid cut from the team," Tom admitted.

"These girls are just so vulnerable. They have the world at their feet, and they don't even know it. Instead they come here and get preyed upon. I hate this world sometimes."

"Don't we all?" Tom said.

DAY 2 -NIGHT

H arri Harper took a left onto Baxter Street off of Silver Lake Boulevard and parked in front of Roxanne Miles' craftsman home.

She had dropped Tom at the PAB and gone back to her desk only long enough to find Roxanne's address and do a quick internet search. Her IMDb page was typical of a working actress with no major roles in any major films. It looked busy for a few years and then, nothing.

She'd gotten lucky because Roxanne lived across from the Silver Lake Reservoir. She could stop by and interview Roxanne on her way home.

Harri checked the time. It was only six-thirty in the evening. She'd made it here in a record time. Roxanne had no idea Harri was coming as she hadn't called ahead. She was taking a chance with that, but surprise interviews often gave her the best information. She lived close enough to Roxanne that she could try to catch her in the morning if she wasn't home.

Roxanne's address had a half number and Harri

discovered she lived in the back house of the lovely craftsman perched on the hill. The view of the reservoir from the home was as good as Harri's. She wondered if Roxanne shared the view, as well.

Harri walked down the paved driveway to the side of the main house, twinkle lights lighting her way to a small gate. She unlatched the hook, opened the gate, and walked into the small, green backyard. The cute guest-house was tucked in the corner. No view but surrounded by a lush flower garden. Harri could smell night jasmine intermingled with fragrant roses, and that other night-blooming flower that smelled incredible, but she had no idea of the name.

Harri pulled out her badge and knocked on the door.

"Who is it?" came a voice from the other side of the door.

"I'm Detective Harriet Harper with the LAPD. I'm looking for Roxanne Miles. Is that you?" she asked.

She held up her badge to the eyehole in the door. The door opened up a crack. A brown-haired woman with large hazel eyes and a tentative look on her face peered out. She was not as young as Harri expected her to be.

"What is this about, officer?" Roxanne asked.

"I'm a Detective. We found an actress dead yesterday. Her name was Sophie Lambert," Harri said.

"I saw the news about that this morning." Roxanne nodded. "I'm so sorry that happened but what does it have to do with me?" she asked.

"May I come inside so we can talk?" Harri asked.

Roxanne hesitated for a moment.

"Please," Harri said. "I won't take up too much of your time."

Roxanne closed the door, unlatched the chain, and let Harri into her home.

First hurdle jumped. Harri gave her a reassuring smile. "Thank you."

"Sure, of course," Roxanne said as she led Harri into the living room "Do you want something to drink? Water or something?" she asked as Harri sat down on the over-stuffed couch. She glanced around, noting a small coffee table and an armchair. Nearly everything was in the shabby chic style. The walls were covered in bookcases filled with fiction books. The TV was paused on Netflix.

"Sorry to interrupt your evening. I'm good, thank you."

"What does this girl's death have to do with me?" Roxanne asked as she sat down in the armchair.

Harri noted her brown hair in a messy bun, and the flowered maxi dress she wore. She thought of Elle Lambert, in almost exactly the same outfit, with almost the exact same expression of weariness. Roxanne looked like she could play an ethereal woman with her long neck, high cheek bones, and curved mouth. She seemed more scrawny than slim, Harri thought.

"A source gave me your name and number," Harri explained. "They believe you could have relevant infor-mation as to what might have happened to her."

The expression on Roxanne's face darkened. Her eyes flashed with anger and Harri worried the woman would kick her out on the spot.

Roxanne's hands balled up into fists. "First that asshole makes me go through my whole story," she spat out her words. "Promises he's going to get this huge piece in the newspaper and expose them all. I wait and nothing happens. It was complete bullshit. He made me tell him every detail of the most horrific thing that ever happened to me, to ever happen to anyone I know and then nothing. Now, he sends YOU and thinks I'm going to put myself through that again? You've got some nerve, Lady."

Her face reddened and Harri could see tears in her eyes.

"Roxanne, I don't know what you're talking about," Harri said carefully. "I am here investigating the death of Sophie Lambert. I'm with the LAPD."

Roxanne pulled herself together somewhat. "Stephen didn't send you here?"

"No. A woman named Helena McCarthy gave me your name. She told us you might be able to help us. Can you tell me what happened to you?" Harri asked.

Roxanne was quiet, lost in her own thoughts. Harri glanced around the room again. There were no photos of Roxanne anywhere. Harri knew that for an actress, that was unusual.

"As long as you promise me you'll do something about it," Roxanne said.

"I won't make you any promises that I can't keep," Harri said. "I need to know what you're going to tell me first."

The two women stared at each other in silence. Harri had no problem with silences and waited her out. Roxanne had not gotten what she'd expected from the journalist after baring her soul and Harri understood that. She hoped if she waited confidently in silence, Roxanne would give her a chance. Finally, Roxanne looked away, down at her hands.

"What's this journalist's name again so I can follow up with him?"

"Stephen Ladner," Roxanne replied in a tired voice. "He worked for the LA Times, or so he said."

Harri wrote his name down. "And what did you tell him?"

Roxanne looked back at her with a cold anger in her eyes. "I told him about the organized abuse of young female actresses," she said.

"Are you talking about the casting couch?" Harri asked.

"I wish that was it," Roxanne rolled her eyes. "No, detective. I was groomed to perform sex acts on powerful industry men. Do you understand?"

Harri was quiet, giving Roxanne room to continue.

"They're organized and prey on vulnerable girls who are just starting out in this industry. It's an entire network. They have a lot of people working for them."

"Grooming?" Harri asked. "Like what a pedophile does?"

"Yes," Roxanne leaned back into the chair. "My therapist explained that to me. I've been working with her since it happened."

"Start from the beginning, Roxanne," Harri said. "I want to hear your story."

Roxanne nodded and took a deep breath.

"I was young and new to town. My home life in Texas was not great. I came out here alone. My first mistake. I was only seventeen. I found myself a manager and he sent me out on auditions almost immediately," Roxanne began.

Harri could see Roxanne's hands tremble. "Do you want to get a glass of water?"

"I'm fine," she said.

"How long ago was this?" Harri asked.

"Five years ago," she said.

Harri looked up at Roxanne. She'd put Roxanne close to thirty or older, not early twenties.

"I know," Roxanne said as if she could read Harri's mind. "I look older than twenty-two. I fell into drugs and alcohol after. Those both age you fast. I'm clean now, but the last three years have taken a toll on every part of my being."

Harri nodded and still said nothing. She waited for Roxanne to continue.

"I was at an audition and this woman comes and sits next to me and starts chatting me up. I tell her I'm starting out and we commiserate on learning our lines and I think nothing of it."

Suddenly, Roxanne jumped up from her seat and went to the fridge in the small kitchen. She poured herself a glass of water and called out to Harri.

"You want any?"

"No. I'm still good," Harri said.

Harri watched Roxanne in the kitchen. She was a jumble of nerves and Harri understood the water was a poor substitute for the alcohol of her choice. She was trying. Harri expelled her breath and patiently waited for Roxanne to continue her story.

"I started seeing her at more auditions and she was friendlier every time. I know why now. That's the first step in grooming. Identify and choose a victim. But I was young. I didn't see it. I was vulnerable and alone. My parents should have never sent me out here on my own, but they couldn't have stopped me."

She gulped down her water and began to pace in front of Harri. "I kept seeing her at my auditions. We became friends. I mean, I stupidly thought she was my friend. She ran lines with me. We'd go for coffee. She said she was an actress and I had no reason to not believe her, to not trust her. That's number two, by the way, in the manual for grooming."

"That wasn't your fault," Harri said. The pain pouring out of Roxanne was almost unbearable to witness. Shame seeped out of her. "You were only seventeen."

Roxanne ignored her. "She invited me to meet a producer on some big action film. She dangled this opportunity for a part. A way to get my SAG card. Every actor at the beginning of their career needs to get their card. She identified my need and provided me with an incredible opportunity. The producer was legit. I knew his name. I'd read about him in the trades. Number three - identify and fill the need."

Roxanne refilled her glass of water and continued to pace. "I agreed to meet with the producer who was charming and nice and gave me a speaking part in his movie. I got my SAG Card. I was thrilled. Thrilled. I thought I was on my way. Like it was really happening for me. Then she asked me to go to a party with her and of course, I wanted to go to a party and rub elbows with a who's who of this town. What girl wouldn't want that?"

Roxanne sat back down in her armchair, her body now limp. "She brought me to that party and I just felt so grateful, so indebted because this woman introduced me to this producer, and I got the part. So, we're at this party with a bunch of faces I've seen on TV and in magazines and she starts asking me to do things for her. All normal like. Like this is an everyday occurrence."

Harri raised an eyebrow. "What kind of things?" she asked, even though she already knew the answer.

"Sexual things with some gross, old producer. I'm shocked and confused at the same time. This is my friend. She's older, and grew up in LA, in the business. So, maybe this is how things happen out here? There was such an air of normalcy about it. Anyway, I declined, and she says 'okay' like it's no big deal. She hands me a drink instead."

"Did she get you drunk?" Harri asked.

"Worse. She roofied me," Roxanne said as she closed her eyes.

Harri knew she was pushing away the horror and she sat patiently for a few moments, giving Roxanne time.

"I came to in the morning," Roxanne continued. "I didn't know where I was, in some room. All I knew was that I'd been raped, but I had no idea by whom."

"Did you report this?" Harri asked.

"Of course not." Roxanne sighed. "That's how they get you. First, she got me a meeting with the producer. Then she paid for some acting classes for me since I was broke, and she was dripping in money. I was indebted. I took advantage of her, right?"

Roxanne's voice comes out fast and hyper. This woman is still clearly suffering from PTSD five years later, thought Harri.

"They see what you need and give it to you," Roxanne said. "Wrapped up in a huge red bow like a miracle from Santa Claus. And then comes the big ask. So, when you do get assaulted, like I did, the shame is just, it's just overwhelming and confusing. I trusted her. I thought she was my friend. I thought she believed in me and wanted to help me succeed. I mean, we talked like we were besties and I told her so much, so many things, and all she did with everything I said was use it to, to lure me. To trap me."

Roxanne paused, breathing deeply to regain her composure.

"I wanted to crawl into a hole and die," she said quietly. "Most days, I still do. Here's the thing, Miss

Lady Detective. So many girls have had this experience. I'm far from being alone."

"How many girls?" Harri asked.

"I don't know." Roxanne shook her head. "A lot. That's what I told Stephen. There's an organization behind all this. It's systematic. They have very specific parties that aren't like your typical Hollywood parties. These are all about showing off new girls for men who have everything…" Roxanne's voice drifted off.

"Give me names," Harri said, her jaw so tight that it was starting to throb.

"No way." Roxanne shook her head. "I'm not sticking my neck out again. These people are powerful. They have unlimited funds. They could destroy my entire life with a snap of their fingers," Roxanne said.

"Roxanne," Harri said carefully. "I want to believe you, really I do. But you know I can't help you unless you give me a place to start. Who was the producer? Do you remember where the party was?"

Roxanne was quiet, looking down at her hands once again. Finally, she looked back at Harri. "I can give you the name of the woman who groomed me."

"What's her name?" Harri asked.

"Georgie Shipwell."

Harri had never heard of the woman before. "You said she was also an actress?" she asked as she wrote in her notebook.

"Her father was Glenn Shipwell."

Harri had heard of Glenn Shipwell. He'd been a famous leading man in the seventies. Had won at least two Oscars from back then. "You told all of this to Stephen Ladner?" Harri asked.

"Yes. I told him even more." Roxanne nodded. "Mentioned some of the famous people I'd seen at the party that night. I could tell he was excited about the story. He called me a week later and told me he'd gotten a big break. I should watch for his article coming out in the next few weeks."

"What happened?" Harri asked. She wouldn't have been that upset with the man if everything had gone according to plan.

"I never heard from him again. The article never came out and when I called him, all he said was his editors killed it."

Harri raised an eyebrow at that. "He said his editors killed the story?"

"Yes," Roxanne said bitterly. "Sound familiar?"

Harri nodded assuming she was talking about the Winegardner case that was currently winding its way through the courts. Winegardner was a famous power agent who apparently had a penchant for raping his clients. His case blew up not only Hollywood, but adjacent industries like Music, Finance and Politics. Industries full of dominant men who like to abuse their power.

"Thank you for sharing your story with me," Harri said. "Do you have any evidence that links you to Georgie Shipwell, or that party?"

"Evidence like what?" Roxanne asked.

"Text messages, email messages, any kind of physical evidence. Do you have the clothes you were wearing that night?"

"No, I don't think so." Roxanne shook her head. "It was five years ago. I had to change my phone, get a new email. I started over. My mom's gone nearly broke with my therapy bills, and I...I honestly just want to forget. I just want my life back."

Harri certainly understood that.

"Roxanne, do you have anything from that night? Your clothes, or?"

Roxanne closed her eyes. "You have to understand. It was all...tainted. I threw it all away. The clothes, the bag, the shoes, the makeup, the necklace, everything. I know I did everything wrong, but I couldn't stop taking showers. I just, I couldn't stop."

Harri was disappointed, but she did understand.

"Do you think that's what could have happened to Sophie Lambert?"

"Was she a teenager and inexperienced?" Roxanne asked.

"Yes, on both counts," Harri said.

"Then she would be perfect," Roxanne said.

"Were there other women who groomed girls? Or only Georgie?" Harri asked.

"I don't know," Roxanne answered. "I only saw Georgie, but I did see her sometimes talking to other girls."

Harri tried to project calmness as she turned the conversation to where she knew Roxanne probably didn't want to go.

"Roxanne, I need you to come down to the station and give a formal statement."

"No, I'm not doing that," Roxanne jumped up from her chair again. "I'm not going down there. I don't want to get involved in this again. I'm sorry about what happened to that girl and I hope you find who did it. But I'm not willing to put my neck out again. Maybe Stephen Ladner did me a favor."

Harri had asked the wrong question, apparently. She closed her notebook as Roxanne headed toward the door.

"I don't really have anything more to tell you," she said. The implication was that she wanted Harri to leave.

Harri obliged and walked to the door. "I understand that you don't feel safe coming out in the open, but I'll need to call you once I dig up what happened with the journalist and what happened five years ago," she said.

Roxanne nodded without saying a word, her big eyes were wide and she looked haunted again.

Harri's heart felt heavy as she made her way back to the car, the twinkle lights a little less twinkly and the darkness surrounding her more oppressive. She knew it had been painful for Roxanne to tell her story, especially after whatever had happened with the journalist. Harri was grateful she'd trusted her enough to try again.

She was glad she was going back to her own home tonight. Jake had said that he'd be over around nine and she was really looking forward to giving him a big hug. She needed someone to chase the darkness away. This case was getting to her and she wondered if she was really ready to get back to investigating. The brutality of crimes could be hard to compartmentalize. Harri worked with empathy and the pain she saw tonight made her want to curl into a ball. It made her a better detective, she thought.

The part of the story that Harri found particularly terrible was that a woman brought her into the fold, manipulated her until she'd gained her trust, and then served her up on a platter to some destructive man.

That thought stayed with her until she arrived back at home.

17

DAY 2 -NIGHT

Debi Mills tugged at her dress nervously and watched as the sleek black car pulled up into her driveway. Her roommate came out behind her and saw the car.

"What's going on Debi?" Janie asked.

"I'm going to my first official Hollywood party," Debi said.

"Wow," Janie said. "You're so fancy."

Debi flushed. "You think this dress is okay?" she asked.

It was one of the dresses she'd brought when she left Arizona and even though it was the nicest thing she owned, she also thought it looked more suburbs and not Hollywood. Georgie had said sparkly, but she didn't own anything like that, so she went with her mint green cocktail dress she'd worn to a wedding a year ago. It was off an off-the-shoulder neckline and hoped it was glamorous enough.

She wondered again if she should be wearing some

sort of vintage ripped T-shirt and skinny jeans with heels, but she didn't own any clothes like that, either.

"You look really nice," Janie said.

"Doesn't look very Hollywood though, does it?" Debi asked.

"What does Hollywood look like." Janie laughed. "It looks like you and that's what matters, right?"

Debi nodded and made a mental note to figure out how to update her wardrobe. The ones she did buy were in the trunk of her car, pressed and cleaned for her auditions. This dress would have to do.

"Wish me luck," she said.

Janie gave her a quick hug and Debi bounded down the stairs. She opened the door to the backseat and found George inside. She waved back at Janie and slid in.

"I love your dress. it's so sweet," Georgie said.

Debi flushed. She couldn't tell if Georgie was complementing her or gently scolding her for not wearing something sparkly. She wanted to run out of the car and spend the night watching movies with Janie. Why had she agreed to even go?

"This old thing? I just threw it on," Debi said in a mock tone. She might as well show that she didn't care either way what Georgie said to her.

Georgie smiled and gave her an approving look.

"Where are we going?" Debi asked. Whenever she went out at night, she would text Janie to let her know where she was going and with whom.

"It's a secret," Georgie said with a wink.

"What do you mean a secret? Are we going into Beverly Hills, Malibu, Hollywood, where?"

"That's part of the fun. It's a secret party and I pulled some strings to get you an invite."

"Thank you for that," Debi said quickly. She was so grateful for everything Georgie had done for her.

"You'll meet some important people tonight," Georgie promised. "You'll book a job after this, I guarantee you. I'll introduce you to everyone I know. And I know a lot of people."

Debi looked nervously out the window. She was excited yet didn't understand why she couldn't tell her the location. Debi decided to try one more time.

"What if I lose you?" Debi asked. "If I don't know where I'm going, then I won't know where to be picked up by a ride share to get home."

"Don't worry," Georgie assured her. "I know this is your first big party. I want to introduce you around, and I'll keep my eye out for you. And you won't need to call a ride share. I'll take you home, silly."

Debi smiled and tried to relax. That strange sense of foreboding came on her again, but she shook it off. She was just in a different pond and needed to learn how to swim in it was all.

She barely knew this woman, yet Georgie had already taken her to a Desmond Ryan class and booked a whole month of private lessons for her. Even though Debi had initially not accepted the offer, Georgie had arranged them anyway.

When she'd texted with the news, Debi wasn't sure how to react. She wished again she had someone to talk to, but she already knew what her manager would say. Take it! She didn't want anyone thinking she was leaching off this rich woman. Lord knew there was enough people in this town like that. At the same time, those lessons could change her life. Why couldn't things be simpler?

Debi bit her lip and looked nervously outside. They

were driving through Hollywood now though she couldn't tell exactly in which direction.

She pulled her phone out of her purse and her stress faded a bit. Her phone had GPS and would tell her the location of the party. Plus, she had a friend-locating app that she'd connected to Janie. She'd text her the address the moment they arrived.

With her solution planned, Debi relaxed and settled back into the seat. Might as well enjoy the ride, she thought.

Georgie popped a champagne bottle open, the liquid frothing out a bit. Georgie let out a little yell and mopped up the liquid with some towels she found in a side compartment.

Debi tried to help her dab at the wet spot, but Georgie shooed her away. "I got this. My fault. I must have shaken it.

"Is that champagne?" Debi asked.

"You look nervous. Let's get you a little bit more relaxed," Georgie said with a laugh and poured Debi a glass.

Debi's heart fluttered but she accepted the drink anyway and took a tiny sip. The sparkly sour taste of champagne flooded her mouth. Debi was being overly paranoid. Tonight, would be a blast, Debi promised herself. She took a longer drink and clinked glasses with Georgie.

It would be a night she'd never forget.

18

DAY 2 -NIGHT

Harri Harper watched as Jake finished eating his pasta dinner in her dining room, the lights low and music playing Miles Davis. If Lauren could see them now, she thought. She wasn't sure what her dead sister would think about this scene. Harri put her hand on her chest like she did whenever she thought about her sister. Jake saw the movement and their eyes met.

"Thinking about Lauren?" he asked.

"Wondering what she would think about us now. We seem so civilized," Harri said.

Jake laughed at that. "I suppose we are civilized now, aren't we?"

"She would find our taste in music objectionable," Harri said with a laugh. Back then her sister was all about punk and ska music. Some of the bands she listened to were from the early 80s, even. She was a surfer girl through and through. So was Jake for that matter.

"I would hope we did some growing up with our

tastes maturing. We shouldn't be listening to the Butt-hole Surfers twenty-five years later," he said.

Now it was Harri's turn to laugh "True enough. And we both became cops," she said.

"Don't demote me! I'm part of the FBI," he drawled in a teasing manner. Their ongoing joke was he'd gone fed instead of being a run-of-the-mill cop.

"Not anymore, Pal." Harri smiled. "You always did have to get fancy, didn't you?" Harri teased him.

Jake finished up the last noodle and washed it down with the Pinot Noir.

"Thanks for the pasta. You don't cook much, but when you do, it's filled with love," he said with a twinkle in his eye.

"You should be honored I'm willing to cook for you," she said and cleared his dishes and her own. He followed her into the kitchen, still gleaming from the housekeeper's visit earlier in the day. She rinsed their dishes in the sink and handed him each one to put into the dishwasher.

"It's good we're making some movement with your FBI resources. I've come up with diddly squat."

"Leonora Dean will come through for us," he said.

"I hope so," she said. "You don't think we're doing this the wrong way by focusing mostly on Jerome Wexler, do you? Maybe we should still be looking for John, Paul, and George. Oh, I totally forgot to tell you something Jackie said. I got lost in this new case of mine. When I saw Jackie, she had mentioned that those were the name of the Beatles. Which kind of goes along with your theory they were fake names to begin with."

"You should always listen to me. I'm always right," Jake said.

Harri jabbed him in the shoulder.

"Ouch, what was that for?" he asked.

"For thinking you're always right," she said.

"Do you want to talk about your case?"

The question wasn't entirely out of left field because she had been really relatively quiet since he'd arrived. Her mind was turning over what Roxanne Miles had told her. She'd set Roxanne off enough to end the interview and her mind was looking at all the angles.

"I met with an assault victim that could potentially be connected to my Sophie Lambert and Addison James case. She claims there's an organization that scouts young actresses, grooms them, and gets them to do things."

Jake frowned. "Like casting couch kind of things?" he asked.

Harri nodded. "She went to some reporter and he'd promised a big exposé, but he never delivered. Claims it was killed by his editors at the LA Times."

"Isn't that exactly what happened with all those Winegardner articles? I'm sure it could easily happen again with another powerful man in the crosshairs of this kind of case. You think that's what Sophie and Addison got caught up into?"

"It's too early to know. My victim said she was drugged. That's consistent with Sophie Lambert. As were the signs of assault. The thing that's making me wonder is the grooming bit. My victim's family didn't live in LA. She was here alone. Sophie's mom is the ultimate stage mom and went with Sophie everywhere. She wouldn't allow that kind of behavior."

"It's a line of questioning you'll have to open with the actresses you'll be interviewing. Didn't you say you have close to two hundred women to speak to?" Jake asked.

Harri nodded and took a sip of her remaining wine.

"I want to start with the journalist first. If he can give me his story, I can use his angle to really hone in on the questions I should be asking. And the people I should be asking about. I scared my victim off, but he got all the names from her."

Jake pulled out his cell phone. "What's his name?" he asked.

"Stephen Ladner. She said he was with the LA Times." Harri hadn't had the time to do any searching on the journalist's name.

"Let's see what he's put out recently," Jake said.

Harri sidled up to him and he drew her to him, the warmth of his body comforting her. When he typed Stephen's name into the browser, a bunch of articles came up under the LA Times. The latest date was eight months ago.

"He hasn't published anything since last December." Jake frowned. "He was putting out articles every week until then."

Jake typed in Stephen's name in the search at the LA Times to see what would come up and found nothing. Next, he found a LinkedIn entry for Stephen Ladner as a journalist that was available for hire.

"Looks like he's without a job now," Jake said.

"That doesn't necessarily mean anything," Harri said. "Journalism has been having a seismic shift and the Los Angeles Times had a huge round of layoffs recently, didn't they?"

"True enough. But I'd go with your instinct of talking to him first to see what the story is behind Roxanne's claims."

"He could have been fired, though."

"Yes," Jake said.

Harri pulled away from him and poured herself some

wine. Her mind skipped to the photos of the look-alike girls.

"You should have seen these printouts of these girls. They all looked the same. I've never seen anything like it."

"What do you mean by the same look?" he asked.

"Like they could have all been twins, Jake." Harri sat back down next to him. "All dark hair, blue eyes, red lips. The vampy sexpot look. They were all vying for some sort of commercial. Did I tell you the reason why one got picked was she was two inches taller than the other? I couldn't believe my ears when I heard that."

"Guess you've never played basketball," Jake said.

"Huh. Tom Bards said that exact same thing," Harri said.

They had finished their wine and Harri could barely keep her eyes open.

"Are you okay if we call it a night a little early? I'm exhausted. I honestly thought once we found Lauren, we'd know what happened to her, but it's just not enough."

"Might never be enough," he said gently.

Harri nodded and put her wine glass on the counter.

"I'm not feeling these stairs," she grumbled as they made their way to the third-floor master bedroom.

"You're always complaining about my stairs," Jake said.

"Your stairs are killer, Jake." She huffed and puffed into the master bedroom and threw herself onto the soft bed.

Jake tumbled next to her. His strong arms folded around her and she melted into him.

"This empty feeling is never going away, is it?" Harri whispered against his chest. "We're working so hard to find the guy and I feel like this emptiness will never be gone. She's gone. They're all gone."

Harri heard a muffled yes in her hair and closed her eyes. She let his warmth calm her. She pulled his hand to her chest and closed her eyes.

This was good.

This would let her sleep tonight.

19

DAY 3 - MORNING

Harri Harper knocked on the door of a beaten-down looking apartment in a run-down building on the corner of Beverly and Wilton.

Stephen Ladner had fallen on hard times. It was a rough neighborhood, quickly gentrifying just to the west, but this part was old decrepit buildings with peeling paint.

Knowing Los Angeles, Harri was sure he was still paying thousands of dollars in rent every month, but she wondered how long he could last in the city without a job. She knocked harder and finally heard sounds on the other side of the door.

The door, however, did not open.

"Who is it?" a man's voice asked from the other side.

"I'm Detective Harriet Harper with the Los Angeles police department. I'd like to ask you some questions," she said.

"I know I don't have to open the door to you," he said. "I don't want to talk to you."

Harri knocked again.

"Roxanne Miles sent me to speak to you. About her story and what happened to it."

"Now you definitely need to go away," he said. "I don't want to talk about that. With anyone. Ever."

Harri bit her lip. It sounded as if Ladner was just on the other side of the door. He was right. He didn't need to open for her. He was talking, though.

"I know your story got killed. You're also out of work," she said.

"Yeah," he said. "I know all that, too. You're an amazing detective."

Harri waited. He wanted to talk. She could tell.

"Roxanne's story did that to me. Thank you for reinforcing why I won't talk to you," he said.

"You know that's what they wanted," Harri said to the door. "To silence you. And you're playing right into their hands. Don't you want to get justice for yourself and for Roxanne and all the other girls this has happened to?"

"I'm a journalist, detective." Stephen said through the door. "I expose the truth. You're the one who's supposed to take it from there. And best of luck with that."

"Thanks, I'm gonna need it," Harri responded with fake cheerfulness.

"You don't think you'll get buried under by this story? What makes you so special?"

"They haven't buried me yet." Harri smiled. "They've tried. Trust me."

"What's your name again?"

"Harriet Harper. I worked the Creek Killer case," she said, knowing he was looking her up on the internet. "And I found my sister's remains up in Oregon, even after the local police and FBI told me to go home."

Stephen Ladner was quiet, still searching she guessed.

"I don't quit," Harri promised.

"These people are more powerful than some small-town cops you've come up against," Stephen said, but his voice sounded closer.

"Look, why don't you tell me your story so I can do what I do best," Harri said. "A young girl was found dead in a wall. I don't know if you saw that, but her case is the one I'm working. Her best friend is still missing but could still be alive. My investigation has landed on your doorstep and I'm not leaving until I speak with you."

The door finally opened a crack. "They murdered her?" he asked.

"Still waiting back on the coroner," she said. "But she didn't get into a wall on her own."

"I want the exclusive," he said. "I gotta make a living, too."

"I'll give you an exclusive once the investigation is done," Harri promised.

"Okay," he said.

The door opened wide and the stench of body odor and cigarettes assaulted Harri's nose. She smiled through her disgust. This wasn't going to be a pleasant interview, but at least she was getting somewhere.

"Thank you for letting me in," she said.

Stephen Ladner was a lanky man with a shaggy beard and unkempt brown hair. And he was tall. Really tall. He stood about six foot five and was thin except for a round potbelly sticking out from underneath his gray T-shirt.

"I hope you're as good as you say you are," Stephen said.

He left the door open and went back into his living room. Harri didn't want to close the door in fear she wouldn't be able to breathe, but he didn't give her much choice.

"Do you think we could open a window in here?" she asked.

Stephen obliged her with a grunt, going over to his desk and sliding a window open.

"Thank you," she said and closed the front door behind her.

Stephen flopped himself down on his sofa, his legs and arms going every which way. The only other seat in the room was the desk chair, piled with manila folders bursting with paper. The desk was covered in files as well. She could see an old mac laptop underneath the smallest stack.

"Mind if I move these?"

"Sure," Stephen said making no move to assist her.

Nice, Harri thought. She grabbed the pile and stacked them neatly on top of the printer. At least, she was near the window now. It had been a long time since she'd encountered smokers in Los Angeles. It seemed everyone was super health conscious here. Stephen had to be a chain-smoker by the smell of this place.

"Why do you think you were fired?" she asked, flipping open her notebook.

"For the record, I wasn't fired. I was laid off weeks before the main layoffs happened."

"That was around seven months ago?" she asked.

"Yeah." He nodded. "I wasn't part of those."

"And you were laid off after submitting your piece?" she asked.

"Two weeks after actually. They thought that was

enough time to not make me suspicious. They were wrong."

"Tell me about your piece. It was more than Roxanne's story?" Harri asked.

Stephen crossed his arms and sighed. "I convinced five women to come forward with their stories. With Roxanne, my article included six women whose stories were similar. Some had photos as evidence and one woman even showed me a video. I wrote up my piece, thinking I was finally on a story that would make my career. I gave it to my editor, and at first, he seemed impressed. They waited 'til the next day to tell me it wouldn't run."

"What reason did they give for not running it?" Harri asked.

"Legal wouldn't approve it," he said with a tight smile. "The men in my piece would most definitely sue. My editor told me the women's stories weren't enough, especially since none of them had ever gone to the police. Two weeks later I was laid off without much explanation."

"That does sound retaliatory," Harri agreed. "What did you uncover in your research for the piece?" Harri asked. The smells in the small apartment were beginning to give her a headache and she didn't know how much longer she could last.

"What's the angle of your investigation?" He came back at her.

Harri narrowed her eyes. He knew damn well she couldn't discuss an ongoing investigation. He was a journalist, she reminded herself. He wanted information for knowledge. What she could say without jeopardizing her investigation?

"I met with Roxanne Miles last night. She gave me

your name. She told me that she was groomed to perform sex acts on wealthy Hollywood power players at exclusive private parties."

"It's so much more than that," he said as a smile crossed his face that looked like a cat swallowing a canary.

He was an unpleasant man who apparently enjoyed playing games with information. Fine, she thought. If he told her what he knew. She would have no problem stroking his ego and telling him how important he is.

"What do you mean?" Harri prodded.

"It's a pyramid scheme," Stephen said, his eyes glinting off the little bit of sunlight coming from the window behind her. He'd leaned forward as he said that. This was the big reveal.

"How so?" she asked.

"The main players get actresses to recruit other actresses. This ensures them getting more girls."

"What do these recruiters get in return?" Harri asked although from what Roxanne had told her she had some idea.

"One of my sources told me they paid her a shit ton of money. Another source told me they'd offered her coveted parts in TV shows and film."

"Were the recruiters abused by these men as well?"

"According to my sources, yes. It made sense with what Roxanne had already told me. Her case was five-years-old and the other girls I spoke to were more recent."

"What did the recruiters offer the other girls?" Harri asked.

"Access," he said with a conspiratorial smile. "What everyone wants in Hollywood."

"Access to whom?"

"To parties, to stars, producers, directors, to the top acting coaches. These recruiters started the grooming process. Once the girls took the bait..."

Shame. That's what made the scheme work. Harri's anger flashed, but she maintained control.

Stephen sighed and continued. "The recruiters are ashamed of what's happened to them, but they see a way out. They just convince themselves it's no big deal. It's the way to win the game. But they know they're serving up other girls to be abused. One of my sources tried to kill herself from the all-consuming self-hatred. It really messes with their heads and makes them ripe for more abuse. It's a vicious cycle. Once they've accepted the money, or the parts in a TV show, they're trapped. It can all be stripped away. They're also complicit. They're part of the machine. So, it's easier to pretend it's just the way things work out here. It's about commitment to their goals, and the money and the clothes and the access and the success are proof that they're making it out here. They've conquered this town. Hollywood didn't destroy them." He shook his head and sighed again.

"How old were your sources when this happened to them?" Harri asked, furiously jotting down notes.

"Two were fifteen, three were sixteen and Roxanne was seventeen. The transactional nature of this whole arrangement was extremely confusing to all of them. We've all heard stories about Hollywood. Everyone laughs about the casting couch. The girls had no idea what was happening and really tried to normalize the abuse so they could go on," Stephen said. His face was filled with disgust and his leg bounced up and down. He'd been affected by it all, too.

"Did you uncover who was running this?" she asked.

"My sources named numerous actors, producers,

directors, and studio execs. Names people not even in the industry would recognize. One of my sources spoke about politicians, too. That's the tripwire I hit in the piece. I doubt some Hollywood studio exec has enough clout at the LA Times to get me fired. But politicians." He shrugged and his voice trailed off.

"Tell me about these parties," Harri said.

"There were passcodes to get in. Very exclusive. Lots of security. The parties must have cost a lot of money, so I think there must have been someone like an admin controlling all of that. There had to be someone who coordinated the event planning, which is a ton of work, and then the security, and the exclusivity. From what I was told, the homes were all over the exclusive neighborhoods around the city and it sounds like they'd use a location for a while, then move on to something else, so that would mean they must have been short-term rentals, or something."

Harri considered what he was and realized he was probably right. He'd been on the story for a long time and had obviously thought about a lot of the behind-the-scenes coordinating that had to have been happening.

"Did any of your sources speak about getting drugged?" she asked.

"All of my sources had been roofied. Alcohol also flowed freely."

"And none of these women went to the police?" she asked.

"That's where the genius of this horrifying little operation comes in to play," Stephen said. "These girls ended up getting acting parts and they would get into classes with well-known acting coaches. Or they'd land a good part in a big movie. If they went public with that, these power players could easily discredit them. It would just be a he said/ she said and then the lawyers would come in with defamation suits, the career would be gone, the connections would dry up, the access would disappear and the public would see them as gold diggers who got what they wanted and then called rape. And that's all before the shame and self-hatred hits. The manipulation in this whole thing is breath-taking. Meanwhile, girls are being assaulted every year."

"How did you convince them to go on the record?"

"They'd all left the business. Gotten therapy and wanted to see their day in court. Brave women, all of them. I failed to do that," he choked out.

"Tell me their names," Harri said.

"No." Stephen shook his head. "I need to call my sources and ask if they still want this all to come out. They need to be prepared."

"What about the recruiters and the organizers? Did you uncover who was behind this?"

"I had names of the men who'd abused the girls. I hadn't uncovered the money trail, though. That was never my strong suit. I could get people to talk to me, but when it came to financials, I'd lose the thread."

"Did your article name these men?" Harri asked.

"Yes."

"Can I have the article?"

"No," Stephen said.

"Why not?"

"It's my insurance policy," Stephen said. "You have enough to investigate. If I give you everything right away, you'll toss me away like everyone else has."

"I'm an LAPD detective. You're hindering an investigation."

"You have nothing to exchange," he said. "I'll just say the article doesn't exist and I was laid off due to budget cuts. If you talk to my former bosses at the LA Times, they'll say the same thing, I bet."

"Stephen, I can't give you an exclusive unless I can close the case. I need the information you have."

He didn't reply but shook head.

"I could get a warrant and take every scrap of paper out of here. Your phone. Your laptop, everything."

"You really think I'm stupid enough to leave all my research lying around here?" he asked her with a toss of his head.

"Fine. Call your sources to see if they'd be willing to speak with me."

"I'll do that today," Stephen promised.

"One last thing," Harri said. She hated leaving without any names, but she could tell Stephen wasn't going to budge on this point. He wanted to be part of the investigation.

"How did this group communicate? Schedule the parties. Tell the girls where to go and who to bring?"

"They did most of the organizing for the parties through Snapchat and Facebook messenger. There were codes for everything, so again. There had to be at least one coordinator somewhere putting it all together. Here's another tidbit for you. All my sources told me there was a lot of video and photos being taken. I'm thinking some of those had to be used for blackmail on some of these wealthier men and the girls, too. It's the perfect scheme to make money from wealthy perverts while having them incriminate themselves. They become beholden to the organization. They're not going to say anything because they know there's dirt on them ready to be released at a moment's notice."

"Did you ever find anyone else who worked in this organization?" she asked. "Caterer's, bartenders, DJ's?"

"Never could find anyone. They must be using their own crew over and over. Which means they probably have blackmail on all of them, too."

Harri stood up. "Call me as soon as your sources reply. I want to speak to them immediately if they're willing to talk."

"Good luck with keeping this case active, Detective."

"What does that mean?" Harri asked, annoyance creeping into her voice.

"I'm betting on you being shut down and fast," Stephen said.

"Not if I have anything to do with it," Harri said.

She left Stephen sitting on his couch, deep in thought and hurried to her car, excitement growing at the information he'd given her.

He'd given her a lot to track down and she had to speak to Tom Bards. She didn't like the fact that Stephen wouldn't give her the names of the men who'd abused his sources, but she hoped the women she spoke to would. What was clear to her though, was he hadn't found the key player to the organization as he called it. If this was a pyramid scheme, who was on top pulling all the strings?

20

DAY 3

Harri Harper walked into the 'Get Your Java' coffee shop on First Street in Little Tokyo. On her way back to the office, she'd gotten a phone call from Tom Bards asking her to meet him there.

This didn't bode well. Was the investigation already in danger, just as Stephen Ladner had predicted? Tom had never wanted to meet outside the office before. A coffee shop wasn't the most private of places and she was unsure of speaking about their cases in public like that. Or could he be getting pressure from Lieutenant Richard Byrne to take her off the case? That was also a possibility.

Harri caught sight of Tom sitting at a table, holding a mug of coffee. She waved and walked over.

"You want anything?" he asked.

"I'm jumpy as it is meeting here. I think I'll wait until I hear what you wanted to talk about it. Wouldn't want to completely jump out of my skin," Harri said, laughing to keep the mood light but secretly terrified by what he would say.

She sat down next to him instead of across from him so they could keep their voices lowered as they spoke.

"Sorry for the cloak and dagger. I didn't mean to worry you, but I wanted to tell you about my meeting with Byrne this morning. As you know, the PAB has ears everywhere," he said.

"Don't I know it," Harri said as her knee started bouncing faster than Stephen Ladner's had earlier.

Tom noticed her discomfort and put her out of her misery. "It's not about you."

That piece of news calmed her almost immediately. "What did he want? I didn't even know he came in so early."

"Surprised me too, to be honest."

"He wants to close us down?"

"Affirmative. He called me into his office and asked me about the coroner's report on Sophie Lambert."

"He doesn't think it's murder?"

"Byrne isn't convinced this should be an RHD case. Thinks it would be better handled by Hollywood Division. Especially since it appears to be a death caused by an overdose."

"She didn't get into the wall on her own, though."

"He wants the case closed or passed on," Tom said. "In the next few days. His exact words."

"So how much time does that give us? We have less than forty-eight hours then?" Harri asked, resentment burning a hole in her gut.

"I've found something to contradict him," Tom replied. "About this being an RHD case. I worked all last night going through records of drug overdoses that fit our criteria."

"The criteria being?" Harri asked.

"Females between the ages of fourteen and eighteen

that died of drug overdoses with ligature marks on their necks. The key criteria was they didn't die of strangulation, but from the drugs."

"You found more girls?" Harri asked in disbelief. Lots of people died of drug overdoses in Los Angeles but the addition of the ligature marks on the neck was too specific to be a coincidence.

"Twelve girls," Tom said and put his hand on hers to quiet her. "I found twelve girls with that criteria. I emailed Grimley with the case file numbers to see if she had more information. All the girls were autopsied because of the ligature marks. It was a surprise finding that none of them died of asphyxiation." Tom kept his gravelly voice low.

Harri checked to see if any patrons were close by. He'd picked the coffee shop well. It was empty besides them and the barista. Some new age music was playing loud enough for them to not be overheard.

"Have you received the toxicology report from Grimley yet on Sophie?" Harri asked.

"No, have you?"

Harri shook her head no.

"What did you have to tell me?" Tom asked.

"Oh boy, do I have a story for you," Harri said. She then told him about Roxanne Miles, how Harri tracked down the journalist Stephen Ladner and his killed story about the pyramid scheme of using and abusing young actresses.

"He wouldn't give you the names?" Tom asked.

"He's protecting his sources. He said he'd call them to see if they'd be willing to talk to us. Stephen refused to give me names of the recruiters or organizers or abusers until he sees our case isn't getting buried."

"His article never came out in any other publications?" Tom asked.

"No," Harri said. "He wouldn't give me anything, either. I threatened him with a warrant, and he said he didn't keep the research in his home."

"Keeping it tight to the chest," Tom remarked and sipped his coffee.

"He wants an exclusive which I promised him."

"Was he fired for doing the story?"

"He believes he was retaliated against for putting politicians into the article."

"But the article never came out," Tom asked, annoyance creeping into his voice.

"He's a worm, but not a slimeball," Harri said, wrinkling her nose at the stench of his apartment. "Smelly too."

"And now I have Byrne demanding we wrap things up. He might have a good reason to be squirrely," Tom said.

"A lot of odd things going on, Tom," Harri said. "I'm used to unseen forces moving the pieces on the chess board, but there are too many things at play on this one." Harri thought again of all the balls Jorge Hernandez seemed to have dropped.

"I'm paranoid myself," Tom said. "And I don't get paranoid."

"The Addison James' case was strange from the beginning. Have you ever heard of someone coming to the chief of police and demanding a specific detective work on the case?" Harri asked.

"No." Tom shook his head. "Highly unusual. Cronyism is a thing. Always has been, but never so blatant before."

"What are our next steps?" Harri asked. "Should we

compile everything and hand it off to Hollywood Division?"

"Hell no. I don't want to, do you?"

"Absolutely not," Harri said.

She was glad to hear Tom Bards was not one of those detectives that toed the line carefully. He was a veteran of the LAPD for over twenty years and must've had his share of politics encroaching onto his cases. For him to be paranoid about this case gave her pause.

"These women need justice," Harri said. "They need their day in court. Start the healing process from the unimaginable horror they've been living through." Harri licked her lips, wishing she'd gotten a coffee after all.

"Harri," Tom said. "We could have a serial killer embedded in this organization. I'm diving further into the twelve girls' deaths. I'll talk to Grimley to see what else she's got. Were the girls being choked as they overdosed? I didn't see that kind of detail in the files. In any case, this pattern should have been discovered way before this."

"That would keep this case with us and RHD?"

"If it's a serial that falls under RHD jurisdiction."

"I'll keep pulling at the threads Roxanne Miles gave me. I have the name of the woman who groomed her. Ladner said he'd give me the names in forty-eight hours. We also have the names those casting directors gave us."

"Might not need him."

"I'll see how far I get with the time we have. I'll keep moving forward without his undisclosed info," Harri said.

"Your boyfriend was a profiler for the FBI at one time?"

"Yes, how did you know about Jake and me?"

"That asshole Special Agent from Oregon spilled the beans on that one. You two really pissed him off."

"Good," Harri said. "He was an ass."

"Sure sounded like it," Tom said.

"Jake's no longer an agent. He does consult work now."

"Even better. We won't have to go through official channels to get his take. Let me put some files together for him. Will you ask if he can look over our case?"

"Of course."

"The little bell above the door chimed and a couple came in, staring at the list of drinks behind the barista.

"Ready to get that coffee to go now?" Tom asked.

"I think I've had enough caffeine for today," Harri said and stood up to go. "I was so pissed at that journalist for withholding his info. Now, I can't believe Byrne is proving his prediction right."

"We won't allow that to happen, will we?"

"No. Were you able to call any of the girls from the auditions," Harri asked as she pulled open the door. Tom threw his coffee cup into the trash and followed her to the door.

"I haven't started. The old files kept me busy. I'll call Grimley again and see if she can squeeze me in today," he said.

As they stepped outside, Tom made a point to scan the street up and down.

"What is it?"

"Have you felt like you're being followed?" he asked.

Harri looked at him strangely. "Come again? My paranoia makes me always hyper-aware. I haven't noticed anything lately."

"Never mind," he said. "Meeting with Byrne this morning started my day wrong. He usually stays away from me. I'm too senior for him to mess with. It doesn't help that I feel like I'm being watched all the damn time."

"When did this start?" Harri asked.

"When we were at the B&B with Sophie Lambert's body. If we've stumbled across an organization as well-funded as this one could be, it wouldn't surprise me to find out we're being watched. It's ballsy as all hell, though."

"We aren't invincible," Harri said.

"That's what worries me." With that grim thought, he waved goodbye and crossed the street to head back to the office.

Harri would work from her cruiser, cold calling as many girls as she could. She hoped she'd be able to meet with some of them today. She was more convinced than ever that Addison James was still alive somewhere. Unless, she'd come across the serial Tom may have uncovered.

Not the time for that kind of thought, Harri said to herself. She didn't want anything to derail her focus. Addison's time was running out.

"Hang in there Addison," Harri said as she hurried back to the cruiser.

21

DAY 3

Harri Harper startled awake with the chiming of her phone. Someone had just sent her an email. It was already four in the afternoon and she must have fallen asleep in the cruiser after her last phone call. She looked over to the lists of girls they'd received from the casting directors. Close to forty had been crossed out.

Harri swiped at the sweat on her brow. How could she have fallen asleep? Then she remembered being frustrated at getting nowhere and closing her eyes to take a break. She must have been asleep for close to a half hour.

None of them wanted to meet as they had barely any contact or no contact at all with Sophie. Harri had asked them all questions about exclusive Hollywood parties and friends coercing them to do things with older men, but none of the girls she'd spoken to so far had any idea of what she was talking about. They sounded genuinely surprised when she shifted to the new line of questioning.

On one hand, that was great news. On the other, she

was frustrated, tired and her mouth felt like she had cotton stuffed in it from all the talking. Her phone buzzed again. The screen said Tom Bards.

She took the call.

"We have another girl missing," he said without any preamble.

"Another missing girl?" Harri asked as she came fully awake.

"The missing girl's roommate walked into Hollywood Division this morning. She said her roommate was a young actress and had gone in a sleek black car to a Hollywood party last night. The girls always text each other when they went out for the night for safety and Debi never did that. Janie, the roommate, could not contact her the entire night. When Janie saw her roommate's bed empty this morning, she reported her missing."

"Wait. This happened last night? It hasn't been even been twenty-four hours yet?" Harri asked, confused, and rubbing the sleep out of her eyes.

"I put out an alert to all divisions about young girls going missing and to contact me even if it hasn't been twenty-four hours. The intake officer didn't take her statement due to policy. He took her phone number and called me instead."

"Can I run with this? I've struck out on the girl's I've called so far," Harri asked.

"Go for it," Tom said and recited the woman's number.

"I'm on it. Good thinking, Tom," she said.

"I wish I'd been wrong," he said.

"Me too. I'll call you when I'm done," Harri said and hung up. She called the roommate immediately and arranged to meet her at her apartment within twenty minutes. It was a fast ride to Morton Avenue in Echo Park.

The apartment was a two-story fourplex far enough from Morton Avenue to avoid the noise. Parking was hard to find, though. Harri circled around the block three times before she finally pulled into a spot several houses away from the address.

The burning sun helped her wake up completely and by the time she knocked on the door, her mind was clear, and she was ready for the interview.

A young brunette opened the door, her face streaked with tears.

"I'm so glad you came," she said in a rush. "I knew the police wouldn't take my report because she hadn't been gone twenty-four hours, but I know something's wrong. Debi would never do this. She's responsible, especially for a seventeen-year-old."

Harri put her hand on her shoulder and said "Slow down and let's go inside. You can tell me the whole story. What's your name?"

"Jeanine Hunter. Call me Janie," she said.

"Thank you, Janie."

Janie nodded and motioned Harri inside. They moved to a white couch in the living room. The apartment was airy with hanging plants everywhere and bright light filtering through the open window.

"What is your roommate's name?"

"Debi. Debra Mills," Janie said.

"Did Debi mention anything about what kind of party this was?"

"She just said it was her first big Hollywood party."

"Did you catch the license plate of the black car?" Harri asked.

"No, I didn't. It was a town car," Janie said, swiping at her face.

"Like a rideshare car?"

"No, like what you see the stars driving in instead of their limos. When they are out on the town," she said.

"Did you see the person inside?"

Janie nodded. "An older woman. Maybe in her late thirties, or early forties."

"Can you describe her?"

"She had a short dark bob, pretty. Debi had been excited because she'd met her at one of her auditions. The woman was some big star's daughter and she invited Debi to some acting coach's workshop. I'm not in the business. I'm a musician so I wasn't paying much attention. Coaching is a scam. It all seems like a way to get money out of all the hopeful artists that come out here."

"Did Debi ever tell you this woman's name?'

"George? Georgie something," she said.

Harri felt a buzzing in her chest. Georgie Shipwell would be the next person she would find and interview.

"Why are you so certain Debi is in trouble?" Harri asked gently.

"We have a pact," Janie explained. "We're both alone out here and we don't have any family. Whenever we go out at night, we text each other the address and who we're going with in case something happens to us." Janie gulped down air.

"Can I get you some water?" Harri asked.

Janie shook her head no. "I've lived with Debi for over a year and she's never not texted me that information. Last night was the first time she hadn't and when I saw she never came home, I knew she was in trouble."

"Do you have her phone number?"

Janie nodded and recited out her friend's number. Harri called and it went straight to voicemail. Either her phone was dead or turned off. They wouldn't be able to ping the phone if it was off.

"Would you mind if I went into Debi's room to see if I can find out who this Georgie woman is?"

"Please. Go," Janie said. "Look anywhere. She didn't know where the party was. When I asked, she told me this woman had said it would be a surprise. She'd let her know when she picked her up."

"We need to track down this woman then," Harri said. "It's a good thing you witnessed Debi being picked up."

"Please find Debi. She's had such a difficult life and she was turning it around. Making it work. It's just not fair," Janie said and began to sob.

Harri sat on the couch until Janie pulled herself back together again. "Can you show me Debi's room now?"

Janie nodded and led Harri to Debi's room. The tiny bedroom was very neat and clean with a twin-sized bed, desk, and a chair. Harri put on her evidence gloves.

Debbie's computer was still on the desk. When Harri opened it, the screen went to a password.

"Do you know what her password is?"

"I don't."

"I'm going to take this with me so the IT department can go through it," Harri said. She took out an evidence bag from her purse and slid the computer inside."

Janie nodded. Harri took a closer look at the cork board on the wall behind the computer.

"Which one is Debi?" Harri asked, peering closer at pictures of young girls in various places in the Southwest.

"The redhead in the middle," Janie said with a sniff.

169

Debi Mills was a gorgeous girl with copper red hair and sparkling blue eyes.

"I'm going to take this photo for her file," Harri said and plucked the photo off the corkboard. "Is the woman in the town car here?"

Janie shook her head no. "She'd just met her last week."

The cork board also contained pictures of large houses, various celebrities at red carpet events and an Oscar awards ceremony.

"That's her vision board." Janie explained.

Harri nodded without saying a word. She looked under pieces of yellow sticky notes with dates and times and a phone number with manager written above it.

"Do you know what these times are?"

"She's a waitress at a diner down the street. Those are her shift times. That's her manager's number," Janie said.

Unfortunately, what Harri was looking for she wasn't finding. Then again that would be too easy. Harri had a first name at least, and a general description to go on. How many rich daughters of famous actors named Georgie could there be?

"Thank you for calling us in. I believe you when you say your friend is in trouble," Harri said.

Janie nodded, seeming to have gone mute.

"Are you going to be okay?"

"I am," Janie finally said.

"If you hear anything from Debi, or anyone calling about Debi, or looking for her, please give me a call immediately." She handed Janie a card with her phone number and email on it.

"I will," Janie nodded. "Thank you for not making me wait forty-eight hours to report her missing."

"Of course," Harri said as she followed Janie back to the living room and to the front door.

"Take care of yourself and make sure to keep your doors locked," Harri said. Janie nodded giving her a small smile.

"I'm sounding like a mom. Sorry. Keep yourself safe as I look for your friend.

She waved good-bye to Janie and hurried back to her cruiser. Her heart was beating hard. The circumstances of Debi's encounter and subsequent disappearance sounded too similar to what Roxanne had told her. She needed to find the connection to Addison and Sophie's disappearances. The grooming portion wasn't fitting in with what they'd found so far. Could Sophie have been groomed without her mother noticing? That was the big question.

She called Elle Lambert.

"Hello?" Elle asked in a tired voice.

"This is Detective Harper speaking."

"Have you found who killed my girl?" Elle's voice came out small and childlike. That didn't sound good.

"We're working on the case of. I wanted to ask you. Did Sophie have any new friends in her life?"

"Not that she mentioned," Elle said.

"Did she receive any new acting lessons? Something that was too good to be true?"

"I got her all her lessons. I'm her…was her manager. I looked after my daughter and didn't need any hand-outs." A note of hysteria was creeping into Elle Lambert's voice.

"Thank you, Mrs. Lambert. That's all I wanted to ask. Take care of yourself."

Harri heard Sophie Lambert's mother sobbing as she hung up the phone. Her pain went straight into Harri's heart. The same place that ached when she thought of her own sister.

Harri clutched her chest as she called Tom Bards.

"Tom, it's Harri," she said into his voicemail. "You were right. Debi Mills was most likely taken by the same people who abused Roxanne Miles. I'm still looking for the connection between Addison and Sophie and this bigger case we've uncovered. Talked to Sophie's mom. She didn't seem to know about any grooming. Debi fits the victim profile. I have a name I'm running down. Georgie Shipwell, who picked her up in a town car on the night she disappeared."

The phone beeped and cut off the call. She'd go back to the office and tell him in person. She didn't have access to the DMV database, or she'd look up Georgie immediately.

22

DAY 3 -EVENING

As soon as Harri pulled out of her parking spot, a black Subaru SUV did as well, several cars back. As she drove towards the 101 freeway, she kept the car in her rearview mirror.

She took a left onto Morton Avenue.

The black SUV did as well.

She merged onto Echo Park Boulevard.

The black SUV did the same.

She was being followed and her shadow had no issue with her knowing it.

Her heart raced faster as she made a swift turn right onto Scott Avenue. She sped up on the small residential street and took the right onto Lake Shore.

The black SUV was attempting catch up but there was too much traffic on Lake Shore. Harri floored at a yellow to take a left onto a small side street. The black SUV got stuck at the light.

Harri kept making lefts and rights on small streets until she hit Glendale Boulevard. She weaved in and out of traffic, putting as much distance between her and the SUV as she could.

They had some balls to tail an LAPD detective, she thought. Her knuckles were white from gripping the steering wheel hard. She would not let panic overtake her. That's what they wanted her to be. Scared. Unnerved. She'd be damned if she'd give them that.

She called Tom again.

"You mentioned something about being followed?"

"Yeah?" he asked.

"I am definitely being followed. Someone was waiting for me outside of Jeanine Hunter's building. When I pulled out, a black SUV followed me. They were obvious about it, too. Either a total amateur or they wanted me to know they were there."

Janie Hunter could be in danger. The thought flashed in Harri's mind. "Call me back," she said and hung up on Tom.

"Crap," she said aloud and called dispatch. She gave them Janie's address and asked for a car to drive by every two hours. Hopefully, the increased presence on her street would let anyone know she was on LAPD's radar. Janie Hunter would be at least good for the night.

Harri drove around for another fifteen minutes in stop and go traffic making sure the black SUV didn't turn up again. She didn't want to lead them to her home. After she was sure the black SUV was nowhere to be seen, she turned onto Silver Lake Boulevard from Sunset and drove up the hill toward home.

The stress and anger drifted away the closer she came. Even though, her home had been broken into some months back by one of the Creek Killers, she worked hard to bring back the peace and joy her home gave her. She'd succeeded in making it her oasis.

Every cop needed a place to let go of the job and her home was that place. The higher her car climbed toward her sanctuary; the more worries drifted away. At least for the night.

That's what she told herself, of course.

The nightmares were back. The ones about her sister and her family. But those were hers to vanquish and had nothing to do with the house. Out in the everyday world, she was a cop. An LAPD detective. In the middle of the night, she was the grieving sister of a murder victim. The personas were both her, different sides of a coin, but she made sure to keep them different sides.

Harri turned right onto her street and slammed on the brakes.

The black SUV was parked right next to her driveway, waiting for her.

She would not allow this.

Harri put the cruiser in park, grabbed her cell phone and threw her car door open. She stormed toward the SUV, taking photos of the man behind the wheel along with the license plate number.

Her move must have unnerved the driver because as she came within range of his car, he started up the motor and peeled away from her, racing down her street.

"I'm coming for you," she yelled at its disappearing taillights.

She contemplated following him but decided against it. If he was so obvious with his intent, she doubted he rolled with stolen plates. She had his plates and face now. That should be enough to ID him.

This stunt felt like intimidation to her. He wanted her to know he was following her, stalking her. Did he and whoever hired him really think she would be scared away because some asshole was staking out her home?

Her body felt on fire as she opened the door and reset the alarm. She stamped down on her anger. Now wasn't the time. She made a beeline for her personal laptop so she could remotely connect to her computer at work. She punched in the license plate of the SUV and the registration came up immediately. The SUV was registered to a private investigator by the name of Darren Westheimer.

"Unbelievable," she said.

Her first call was to Tom. His phone went to voicemail. Where in the hell was he?

"That black SUV belongs to a PI and he was sitting out in front of my house just now when I got home. He wanted me to see him. PI named Darren Westheimer. Call me back."

She hung up and checked the time. Her shift was officially over, but a girl was still missing. She did a general search for a George or Georgie Shipwell in Los Angeles but came up empty. She tried more variations of the name, but nothing showed up. Could the name George be a nickname? Or a middle name?

Dammit! And here she thought she'd gotten lucky. She left her computer connected and went to the kitchen to get some water.

How else could she find this woman? Having a famous father should have made it easy, but nothing about his biographies that she could find online mentioned a daughter, or even a son.

Maybe Roxanne Miles knew her? She called Roxanne but also got voicemail.

Irritated by not being able to reach anyone, Harri took a break and dug around the refrigerator for something to eat. She found some tortillas and cheese and made herself a quesadilla.

She tried calling Roxanne Miles again. Harri left another message asking her to call back.

She went back to her computer and did more general searches on different variation of George and Georgie, spelling them every way she could think of. After an hour, she gave up on that as well.

Her thoughts returned to Debi and Addison. The two girls didn't have anything in common outside of their ages and beauty. Janie was attractive and young, as well.

She'd led the PI straight to their apartment. Whomever hired Westheimer might think Janie knew something for a cop to be seeing her so quickly after Debi's disappearance. She should have more protection, Harri thought. A uniform sitting in front of her house for the night, at least. Should Harri call Janie and tell her to stay put? That would only scare her and for what purpose? Harri wasn't sure of anything at this point.

Harri made one last phone call to dispatch and asked for a car to sit on Janie's address saying she'd been threatened by a private investigator and her witness might be intimidated. Dispatch sent a unit to Janie's apartment and Harri breathed in relief.

Lieutenant Richard Byrne would not be happy about her not getting permission, but she didn't care. She believed Tom Bards would agree with her assessment. If she could've reached him, she would have asked. She'd have that fight with them tomorrow morning.

As it stood, no one had called her back. Including Jake.

Harri sat down at her desk and stared down at the lists of actresses she still needed to call. She placed the evidence bag of the photo of Debi between two smiling girls.

Exhaustion washed over her. She closed her eyes.

Just for a moment.

Harri sprinted through the dark woods.

Twigs crackled behind her.

The heavy breathing was getting closer.

RUN! Her mind screamed at her.

She picked up her knees higher and pumped her legs as hard as she could.

Why did it feel like she was running in place?

Branches slapped her face and she caught the full moon behind the thick canopy above her.

She was in Oregon. On the island. She was sure of it.

The sounds of her pursuers grew more distant. She turned to see if she could make out anything in the darkness.

Big mistake.

Her foot caught on a tree root and she went flying into the air.

She hit the soft earth with a small thud, her mouth open in a silent scream.

She tasted something foul.

Something familiar. She spit out whatever was in her mouth and gagged.

Harri pushed hard into the softness underneath her to propel herself back to kneeling.

She saw what she had tasted. It wasn't earth.

She was in a grave.

Her sister's grave, her desiccated body underneath her.

Harri threw back her head and screamed.

She startled awake, gasping for air. She'd fallen asleep on the list of women she needed to call; Debi's evidence bag stuck to her cheek. She pulled it off gently with shaking fingers.

She checked the time and saw it was close to midnight. No calls from anyone, either. Harri dragged herself to her feet and rubbed her tongue on her shirt sleeve trying to get the taste of death out of her mouth.

The nightmare had disappeared in the last few weeks. It was back now. The missing girls must've triggered it again.

Why did it always have to be girls? Why so many of them?

She climbed the stairs to her bedroom and went straight to the bathroom. The familiar buzz of her toothbrush couldn't shake the dream off. She still tasted death.

Should she call Jake?

It was late but she knew he would come if she asked him to. No. She would handle this alone, like she had for the last twenty-five years. This was her burden to bear. She was a cop and needed to pull it together. She would not be too late for those girls.

They were alive somewhere in this city. They would find them. They had to. She had to.

23

DAY 4

Harri Harper woke up at four in the morning like she had all week and was back at her desk in the Cold Case unit by six. She liked the office at this hour. The quiet helped her get more work done.

When she researched the PI, who'd been following her further, she found he was connected mainly to the movie studios and celebrities. He sounded like a fixer to her.

This information, of course, helped pinpoint what case he was working, Harri thought dryly. She'd put in a request for camera footage from the nearest traffic lights to Janie and Debi's apartment to see if she could find the town car that picked Debi up.

With that done, and taking a cue from Tom, Harri had spent the rest of the morning checking the names of the girls the casting directors had given them against any open cases to make sure they were all accounted for.

Nine o'clock rolled around and people began to filter into the office. Harri was about to start calling the actresses again when Tom's head appeared around the wall of her cubicle.

His mouth was set in a thin line and he did not look happy.

"Thanks for calling me back last night," she said.

He didn't respond except to nod toward the hallway.

"What is it?" she asked.

"Byrne wants to see the both of us," he said. "At first, he wanted to see only me, but I want to make sure you're there to witness this."

His tone made Harri frown. "Are you saying what I think your saying?"

Tom nodded. "Grimley called me last night and left a message. By the way I got all your messages, too."

"I left a lot them. Sorry." Harri said as she walked with him to Byrne's office.

"I should have mentioned I would be unavailable last night. I promised my son I'd take him to a baseball game, and he made me shut off my phone."

Harri nodded, understanding.

"Is Grimley's call the reason we're being summoned?"

"I think so. She's ruling Sophie Lambert's death a myocardial infarction due to ingestion of illegal substances."

"Heart attack," Harri said as she followed Tom into the elevator.

"It's not murder."

"Which means not important enough for RHD." Harri sighed.

"Sophie's case is going to Hollywood Division. I'm sure of it."

"What about the serial killer you've uncovered?

Didn't she have ligature marks on her neck, too? Didn't Grimley notate that in her findings?"

"I'll bring that up. I doubt it will fly, though."

"What drugs did she ingest? Was it just the Fentanyl and heroin?" Harri asked as they headed to the elevator let them out.

"Fentanyl and heroin. Grimley confirmed the dose itself didn't kill her. It would've incapacitated her pretty darn good. Her undiagnosed heart condition was activated by the drugs and caused a heart attack."

"How'd she get into a wall? Does Byrne think she wrapped herself in plastic and crawled into a wall and then sealed herself up as she was experiencing a fatal heart attack?"

"Byrne said yesterday a freaked-out dealer. He's grasping at straws." Tom scowled.

"But why a wall? Why didn't they drop her body on the street?" Harri asked.

"That's exactly what I want to ask Byrne," Tom said. "It won't matter. He wants to use RHD resources for bigger crimes."

"What bigger crimes are there than a seventeen-year-old girl being fed drugs, raped repeatedly, and her dead body stuffed into a wall?"

"You can ask him that question yourself," he said.

Harri sighed. This was going to be an ugly meeting.

Tom strode into the RHD bullpen and went straight to the lieutenant's office with Harri in tow.

Harri had managed to avoid seeing Richard Byrne in six months and that was the way she liked it. They tussled about twelve years ago and he'd never forgiven her supposed insubordination.

Even now, he kept trying to derail her career however he could. He was a cheap-shot kind of guy.

Byrne stared at them from above his reading glasses, his eyes narrowing when he saw Harri.

His look of displeasure matched her own, she was sure of it. Harri shot a glance at Tom who had grown still, his eyes taking in everything. He was a formidable man in this moment, Harri thought.

Could Tom have invited her to this meeting as a distraction? A way to throw Richard Byrne off his game enough to get what Tom wanted out of him? She wouldn't put it past him.

"You wanted to see us, Richard?" Tom asked.

"I wanted to see you. You insisted on bringing her," he said with a sneer.

"This case is both of ours. We've done a lot of leg work on it. If anything changes, Harri should be included in that information."

"I need you to close this case and hand it off to whoever's working drugs in the Hollywood division. We don't have RHD resources for a case like this."

"Don't you think the death of a seventeen-year-old girl and two current missing girls should warrant RHD resources?"

"As I'm sure you are aware, RHD only takes on specific cases. This crime, while terrible, is not in our purview and the detectives at Hollywood should have no problem investigating it and bringing the drug dealer to justice."

"There's another young girl still missing. From what I understand, her father knows a lot of people," Harri reminded him.

"You are in Cold Case and Lieutenant Violet Howard deals with you. If she's okay with you still looking at the Addison James case, that has nothing to do with me. As of right now, Tom, I am ordering you back to work on the bank robbery task force."

"I've uncovered twelve girls with supposed over-doses over the last five years with the same combo of fentanyl and heroin in their system. Each victim had light ligature marks on her neck, but asphyxiation was not what killed them. That's a signature," Tom said, keeping his voice cool and even. "Last I knew, RHD took all the serial killer cases in LA County."

Richard sat back and now Harri understood what Tom was doing. He inferred they had another serial killer on their hands. One that had gone undetected for the last five years and whose last victim was Sophie Lambert.

"That could be a coincidence," Richard said, sounding unsure now.

"Whose idea was it to close this case down?" Tom asked.

"Came from Chief Atkins. Straight from the top," Richard said. "My hands are clean on this one. He demanded we put all resources to the spate of bank robberies in the valley. We created a task force yesterday. He wants all hands-on deck."

"And if there is a serial killer preying on young teenage actresses?" Tom asked.

"That's a different case for now. I can say you're off the Sophie Lambert case for the time being. You connect these girls and find a way to prove it's the same guy, and I'll bring the case back."

"I can still work the case then?" Tom asked.

"You're working the potential serial killer case that you just brought to my attention," Richard said testily.

"Got it. Thank you, Lieutenant," Tom stood up and walked out of the office with Harri close behind.

"Did I keep him on edge enough?" she asked Tom.

Tom laughed out loud. "Yes. You did great. I figured you'd see the play. Richard Byrne doesn't do well when he's off balance. Forgets his political maneuvers. On my own, he would have steam rolled through my request. You're his kryptonite. It's amazing how much he hates you."

"The feeling's mutual," Harri said. "And good to know in case we butt heads again."

"I'm still being followed, by the way. I noticed a black SUV following me after I dropped off my son at his mother's house. We've rattled some important man's cage and he's coming at us with what he's got."

"Getting to the Chief of Police is something big," Harri observed.

"It takes chutzpah to follow LAPD, too. They didn't do their research though, did they?"

"What do you mean?"

"Intimidation only works when you have something to lose. You worry about your family, your career."

"We don't have much to lose, do we?" Harri finished.

"My kids are grown. I'm divorced and live alone. Don't even have a dog."

"You have a career?" Harri asked.

"I could retire tomorrow with my full pension. Got no aspirations for more. What about you, Harri?"

"I want the truth at whatever cost," Harri said.

"That's what I mean. They didn't do their proper research on us."

"Or they're desperate which never bodes well," Harri said thinking of Debi and Addison. It was going on four weeks that Addison had been missing.

"We need to go talk to that journalist of yours. Think we can set up a meeting with him like right now?"

"Instead of calling, let's just go there. I don't think he leaves his place much. You can play the bad cop and we can pressure him to give up what he knows," she said.

"I like the way you think," Tom said.

Harri smiled as she went to grab her things.

24

DAY 4

D ebi awoke to fuzzy light streaming out of one barred window. She had no idea how she got here, but she hurt bad. Inside. She'd been a virgin before this and had a feeling she no longer was. A sob escaped from deep within her.

She squeezed her legs tight against each other and felt tears roll down her cheeks. Her head hurt so badly, and her mouth tasted dry and scratchy. Swallowing was hard. She needed water.

How did she get here? Where was here?

Whose clothes was she wearing?

Where were her bra and underwear? Her good dress?

Her body ached so bad and the scratchy material of the red shirt chafed against her skin. The black boxers were loose around her waist and falling off from the worn elastic band.

The dress she'd been wearing, her bra, and underwear were gone. When she looked at her arms, she saw bruises around her wrists. Debi lifted herself to a sitting position and her vision swam.

Oh my God, her head hurt so bad. The last thing she remembered was drinking the champagne with Georgie. Could she have roofied her?

The thought confused her.

Georgie had been so kind to her. Her gut roiled with vomit and she knew she'd made a terrible mistake. Debi curled up into a fetal position and waited for the nausea to go away.

She must have fallen asleep again because when she came to, she was up against the wall in the narrow bed. Debi knew she had to get out of this room.

She sat up again and attempted to take a step. Her leg felt like jelly and crumpled beneath her.

Sobs reverberated around the room in an echo. It took a moment for Debi to realize she was the one making those harsh guttural sounds.

Get up.

GET UP! Her mind shouted at her body. Using the bed as a crutch, she placed both feet on the ground and used every ounce of willpower she had to get to standing.

Bile rose into her throat and she swallowed it down.

Take a step. Her legs shuffled forward. The movement made her woozy, but she kept at until she made it to the window.

Debi pulled the gauzy white curtains back and stared at a wall of trees with a dirt wall behind them. She'd seen this kind of house before.

Janie and she'd had cheap fun sometimes on the weekends going to open houses pretending they were a lesbian couple looking to buy a home. They'd munch on the free snacks and pretend to be house hunting. They'd seen some stilt homes where one side of the house was built into the hillside.

Her phone.

Where was her phone? Had they taken it away from her along with her clothes?

She patted the bed for any hard objects, but it was all soft and lumpy. They would never leave her phone behind. Debi knew she'd been a stupid girl. She was going to pay for that stupidity a thousand times over.

She gingerly sat on the bed, her body broken and bruised, and sobbed. She sobbed for the naive girl she'd been. Sobbed for her body. Sobbed because she didn't know what else to do.

Two years. She'd made her life in Los Angeles for two years and she'd been happy, for the first time in her short life. And now?

Was she going to die here?

There were fates much worse than death, a small voice whispered in her mind. You are going to wish you were dead.

Debi pushed the voice away. She wasn't going to despair. Not yet. She turned to the door and found herself staring at a small black hole above the door jamb.

She slid off the bed and lurched to the door to get a better view.

The hole was glass and if she looked at the right, angle she saw the lens behind it. Whoever had her, had taped her misery.

Debi wasn't tall enough to get a better look at it. Instead, she flicked the camera off. Then smiled.

She spit on her thumb and then standing on her tip toes, her body screaming in the most excruciating pain, smeared the glass with her spit.

To hell with them. Debi Mills was going to survive

this somehow and get the hell out. A spark of fury ignited deep within her soul. She nurtured it and fanned its flames.

She would get out of here or die trying.

25

DAY 4

arri Harper parked in front of Stephen Ladner's apartment building and pointed to the second floor.

"His apartment is right there," she said.

"Some rough digs," Tom said, squinting against the morning light up to the second floor. "Maybe we should have called."

"I'm telling you; the guy doesn't leave the place. Prepare yourself for the smell," Harri said as she exited the cruiser.

"Can't be that bad," Tom said as he followed her into the building.

"Hope you're okay throwing out that fancy suit."

"He's a smoker?"

"Chain smoker," Harri said as they climbed the stairs to the second floor.

"He's unemployed still?"

"That's what he told me."

Harri banged on the door like she had the last time.

"Stephen Ladner. It's Detective Harriet Harper with the LAPD," she yelled.

They waited a moment. The door stayed shut.

"We don't have probable cause if he doesn't open up," Tom said.

Harri tried the doorknob. It was locked. She banged on the door until her fist hurt. The racket finally brought out Stephen's next-door neighbor. The woman was in her forties with rollers in her hair, wearing a vintage-style waitress uniform. Harri thought she either worked at one of the retro diners in town or could also be an actor getting ready for a day of work on set.

"You police?" she asked in a gruff Brooklyn accent.

"LAPD," Tom said. "Is Stephen home?'

"And where were you last night?" she demanded.

Tom and Harri gave her their full attention.

"What do you mean?" Harri asked.

"There was a big fight over there last night," she said.

"What time?" Tom asked, flipping open his notebook.

"Around one in the morning. My bedroom is against his living room and I could hear voices and thumps all night."

"Did you call the police?" Harri asked.

"I called the nonemergency number and reported a fight. I didn't want him to get in any more trouble."

"More trouble?" Tom asked.

"He's in a spiral," the neighbor said. "Things just keep going from bad to worse for that guy."

"How many people did you hear in there?" Harri asked.

The neighbor crossed her arms over her chest and leaned against her doorjamb and sighed.

"Sounded like three guys? Stephen and two others. At first it was just loud voices and then, I don't know.

Like things getting knocked over. I heard Stephen shout 'stop' and 'get out'. This was late, and I had to take one of my pills to get some sleep. I know I heard Stephen laughing at one point and then, I don't know."

"What do you not know?" Tom asked impatiently.

"I think I heard Stephen scream, but I don't know. I was drifting off to sleep. I could have just dreamed it."

"Have you seen or heard him this morning?" Harri asked.

"No," she said. "It's been quiet since I've been awake."

Harri looked at Tom. "We just got our probable cause," she said.

Tom nodded. "Who's the property manager here? We're going to need to get into that apartment," he said.

"Oh, that's Matthew Harold," the neighbor said. "He's downstairs. I can get him for you."

"Yes, do that." Tom said.

She left Harri and Tom standing at Stephen's door and disappeared down the stairs.

"That's not good news," Harri said, biting her lip.

"Let's hope he's still alive," Tom said.

If Stephen had been in a drag out fight with two men, Harri doubted he would have come out the winner. No question what they were looking for.

Matthew Harold, a portly man with a receding hairline approached them carrying a bunch of keys.

"Roberta says your finally here about the ruckus last night," he said.

"You heard the fight, too?" Harri asked.

"Whole damn building heard it, probably."

"Why didn't you call 911?" Tom asked, exasperated.

"Stephen's not a bad guy, but he's got a mouth on him. Especially when he drinks, which he's been doing a lot of lately. He's had his problems since he lost his job and the last thing he needs is to be arrested," Matthew Harold said.

Roberta the neighbor shook her head emphatically at that and Harri had to really hold her tongue and not snap back a nasty remark. How were they supposed to help people if they didn't know they were in trouble?

Matthew pushed past her and unlocked the door for them.

"Please stay outside," Tom asked politely.

Matthew and Roberta nodded and huddled in front of her open door.

Tom and Harri stepped into Stephen Ladner's living room. The room had the familiar smell of cigarette smoke and body odor. Another new smell blended in with them. It was one that unfortunately Harri knew well.

The smell of death.

"We're too late," she said.

Tom picked up the smell, too. He dialed headquarters as they carefully picked their way through the living room into the bedroom.

"Oh no," Harri said.

Stephen Ladner, all six-foot-five of him, hung from a rope tied to a metal bar in his bathroom doorway. Harri found it surprising the bar was able to hold all his weight. Yet, it did.

His face was purple, and his swollen tongue protruded grotesquely out of the side of his mouth. The sickly sweet smell of alcohol and nicotine leaching from the body mixed with the very beginning stage of decomposition was causing the putrid stench.

"It's Detective Tom Bards. I need units, coroner, and CID to 18975 Wilton Place, Apartment 23. Detective Harriet Harper is on scene. Suspicious death."

They listened to the radio squawking as dispatch sent the requested units. Harri picked her way through the living room back to Roberta and Matthew Harold still standing outside.

"Could you please go back to your apartments for now. Unfortunately, we have a body in there," she said.

Roberta gasped and her hand fluttered to her mouth. She turned pale as Harold took her other hand.

"We'll need to take your statements. Will you be able to hang around for a while?

"Oh, I should have called 911," Roberta said. "Why didn't I call 911?" she asked and hurried back to her place, closing the door behind her.

Matthew Harold looked like he was going to be sick.

"Is it Stephen?" he asked.

"Do you know if Stephen Ladner had any next of kin?" Harri asked. She had met Stephen and could make the ID, but it was preferable to have a family member do it.

"Not that I know of," Matthew Harold shook his head. "I'll check the lease."

"Thank you. What apartment are you in?" she asked.

"Number one, downstairs."

"We'll be down to speak with you soon."

When Harri finished with Matthew Harold, she returned to the living room, putting her gloves on to make sure she didn't contaminate the crime scene.

"I'm not seeing a computer in here," Tom said.

"He had files all over the desk and chair when I saw him yesterday."

Tom turned to the empty desk. "That desk?"

"I couldn't have told you the color of the wood from

all the files stacked on that desk. There was a laptop and a printer, too."

"Whoever was in here did a thorough clean-up job, Tom said.

"See a phone anywhere?" Harri asked.

"Nope," Tom answered as he looked in the bedroom. "No phone. CID is on the way to do their thing. If it's in here, they'll find it."

Harri sighed heavily. This case was becoming such a scramble. She hated thinking ill of the dead, but she wished again that Stephen Ladner hadn't tried to outsmart everyone. He thought he'd play games and win, but he wasn't winning any games now.

"Could this be a suicide?" Tom asked.

"The man I spoke to was definitely not suicidal," Harri said. "He wouldn't commit suicide by hanging, either. He'd pop some pills. Hanging takes effort and determination. This guy was lazy, feeling sorry for himself. What I could see him doing is calling someone who had a lot to lose to blackmail them."

"He was that desperate?" Tom asked.

"Definitely," Harri said. "Sounds like his neighbors thought so, too. How would you go about hanging someone that tall?

"Well, it was me, I'd come behind him and choke him unconscious first. Get him incapacitated, so he's easier to handle. Then I'd drag him over to the bathroom and hoist him up. We'll have to see if the rope is his. Doubt his friends would have brought one with them."

Harri stood next to Tom, looking at what was left of Stephen Ladner. It was times like this that Tom's experience really made itself evident. He could look at a crime scene and easily imagine how it all came together.

"What if they drugged him first? Then you'd only need one man."

"Good point. Without drugging, I think it would take two men."

"Why?

"One of 'em had to be at least as tall as me," Tom nodded. "Otherwise they wouldn't have been able to hoist him up and pull the rope around him."

Harri nodded. "Stupid."

"Talking about him or yourself?" Tom asked.

"Both of us," Harri said. "Him for playing games and not giving up his information. Me for not putting protection on him."

"Protection from whom, Harri? We don't have the full story. He refused to help us, remember. I'm not sure what you could've done to help him," Tom said.

Harri didn't respond. She had another death on her conscience and focused on filing that away to be dealt with later.

"He could have been drugged, too. Made him compliant enough to put that noose around his neck and string him up."

"The use of the noose. It's a unique way to kill someone," Tom said.

"Like the girls."

"Except the girls didn't die from the noose. The drugs did him in. By the look on Stephen's face, he died by hanging,"

Sirens sounded off in the distance, getting closer with each passing minute. The apartment would be crawling with the investigative team soon enough.

"I need to call Byrne." Tom said with a tone of displeasure. "You need to go find Roxanne Miles."

"He's cleaning up his trail," Harri said. "I'll get her a protective detail."

"We need her to give us names," Tom said. "If Stephen Ladner died over that expose, she's definitely next."

"I'll call you as soon as I get there," Harri said and rushed back to the car, phone already in hand.

She shouldn't have let Stephen Ladner call the shots. She should have called his bluff and come with a warrant that same day. Harri wondered if the men following her had been monitoring Ladner first. They couldn't have known he gave her nothing. They would have assumed that he'd given her everything. Harri thought about what he'd said about not keeping the information in the apartment. She hoped that meant they'd gotten nothing out of Stephen Ladner.

Except his life.

Had Stephen made himself a target by trying black-mail? Harri couldn't put it past him. He was an arrogant ass who really thought he had an ace up his sleeve. Where was that ace now? What had he done with all his research? These people had proven they would stop at nothing to keep the story buried, by any means necessary.

Harri clenched her hands around the steering wheel as she drove too fast to Roxanne's house. Guilt and anger danced a jig in her mind. She jammed her foot on the gas and raced through traffic. She would not make the same mistake twice.

"Hang on, Roxanne. I'm coming," Harri said aloud.

DAY 4

J ake Tepesky arrived five minutes early for his interview with Ruby Collins, an executive at a production company called Ultra Entertainment. He discovered Jerome Wexler had invested in a film in the early nineties. Jake had spent a day researching the film to find all the major players on the film for him to interview. He hoped to start with any above-the-line women first because they would have a better read on a man like Jerome Wexler as opposed to a male producer who'd brought him on. Ruby Collins fit the bill.

The Ultra Entertainment production office was in Santa close to the pier on Second Street. Jake rarely visited Santa Monica and when he stepped out of the parking structure, he inhaled the salty air and his days as a carefree surfer came flooding back. He hadn't surfed since Lauren disappeared. He couldn't stand to be near the ocean because thoughts of what Lauren endured nearly broke him.

He focused on setting aside his rage. He stood next to

his car and took three deep breaths to center himself. Then he smiled to no one to set himself for the task at hand. Jake took the stairs two at a time to the third floor where the production offices were.

He opened the door to the smell of coffee and dough-nuts, making his mouth water. The office was a light and modern open floor plan, filled with film posters and décor. Most of the staff he could see were young and obviously stressed. He stood and listened to two unseen girls on the other side of a cubicle wall arguing over a script, going point by point through a scene. Jake squeezed his eyes shut at the sound of their voices and pushed thoughts of young lives brutally ended out of his mind.

He approached the receptionist. "Jake Tepesky here to meet with Ruby Collins," he said.

Jake had learned years ago that most people in Holly-wood got excited when he mentioned he was previously with the FBI. Especially the writers and creative execu-tives. Enough movies and books about serial killers were popular to make his former job sound exciting and exotic. If they only knew what true horrors still haunted his mind.

A dark-haired woman with a big smile came from the hallway behind the receptionist. Jake observed her as she approached him. She was petite and wore a hot pink and orange sweater with white capri pants and heels. She was tiny like a bird and, even though she looked to be in her late forties, Jake guessed she'd had some work done and was closer to early sixties. That age made more sense if she'd been executive producing films in the early nineties.

"I'm Ruby Collins. Jake Tepesky?" she asked.

"The one and only," he said as he shook her hand.

"Thank you so much for taking the time to meet with me."

"It's not every day I get to meet an honest-to-goodness FBI profiler. Are you a writer?" she asked as she motioned for him to follow her.

Jake laughed at that. "Nobody's ever asked me that question before," he said.

"When I told a friend of mine, I was meeting with a former FBI profiler, she wanted your name and number immediately," she said.

She took him over to a small conference room with a beautiful view of the Pacific Ocean. The room also displayed two Oscars and several Emmys.

"Congratulations on your awards," he said as he took the seat adjacent to hers.

"Thank you," she laughed. "After close to thirty years in this crazy business I'm glad I finally got some shiny gold statues. Makes me feel so grown up." Her laughter was deep and throaty.

Jake liked her immediately.

She motioned to a coffee maker and water pitcher filled with lemon water on the credenza behind them. "Would you like a coffee or water?" she asked.

"Neither. Thank you."

"You wanted to talk about the production of The Last Spy?" she asked.

Jake nodded and opened his notebook.

"I'm actually more interested in one of your financiers, Jerome Wexler. It looks like it was the only movie he ever invested in," he said.

"Oh, wow." Ruby smiled tightly. "Blast from the past. What do you want to know about Jerome?" she asked.

"Who brought him into the project?" he asked.

"The director Bryan Mortimer. You know who that is, right?" she asked.

"I watch the Oscars, occasionally. He's one of the biggest directors for, what? The last twenty years at least?" Jake asked.

"That's him now," Ruby said. "Back then, he only had one movie under his belt, and it was a moderate success at Sundance. For some reason, the agents and execs at the festival that year fell in love with him. They anointed him as the next big thing. There was a huge bidding war for his movie. The company I worked for at the time offered him a huge pay bump to direct his next movie, *The Last Spy*. It was about a disgruntled spy and a bank heist. Did you see it?" she asked.

"A long time ago," Jake admitted.

"Bryan wanted to bring Jerome Wexler on because he was some sort of finance guru. He also wanted Jerome as a consulting researcher because the film had a financial bend to it. Jerome decided he liked the script so much he wanted to invest in it, becoming the largest investor outside of the studio."

"Do you know how much he invested?" Jake asked.

"Not offhand, but I should have the financials some-where. I could send them to you," she said.

"I would appreciate that," Jake said. "What was Jerome Wexler like?"

"Oh, Jerome." Ruby rolled her eyes. "He thought he was the smartest guy in the room. No matter which room. He was charming, thought he was way more attractive than he actually was. He threw his money around like nobody's business. He was one of those producers that wanted the fame. He wanted to be at the premiere, be seen with all the actors, and mingle with all the famous Hollywood people. He was the kind of producer who wanted his ego stroked. Constantly. Didn't really seem to care about making money from it, even though he eventually did make a nice return."

"Did he come off as creepy at all?" Jake asked.

"Oh, I don't know," Ruby said. "It was a long time ago. Way before #metoo happened. Things used to be different. There was really no such thing as sexual harassment. I mean, it existed. But it wasn't called that. There were no seminars from HR about it." She laughed again. "I mean, if the guy was attractive enough, we thought they were compliments." She shook her head.

Jake shook his head, too.

"Why are you asking if he was creepy?" she asked, her eyes sharp and observant.

"He was head of a pornography ring up in Oregon."

Ruby's mouth fell open and her eyes went wide. "Pornography? Oh, my God," she said. "Oh, my god. I never heard anything about that."

"It didn't hit the papers because he left the country before he was charged," Jake explained. "Did you know he tried to run for governor of Oregon?"

"That ego of his." Ruby rolled her eyes again. "I don't remember anything about that, but he was charming enough to be a politician."

She sat back and regarded Jake with a glint in her eye.

"What are you not telling me, Mr. FBI Profiler? I can smell a story on you, but you're being very cagey about it," she said.

"It was child pornography, Ruby."

Jake was quiet as her mouth fell open again. He gave her a moment to process what he was saying.

"It appears he also ran a camp for underprivileged

children, which was used as a pornography studio and gathering place for pedophiles."

Ruby looked aghast. "Oh, my God," she said again. "Seriously? That's so horrifying. Oh, my God."

Jake gave her another moment to process the information.

"And he was never caught?" she asked.

"He slipped out of the country on a private jet, never to be heard of again."

Ruby turned pale and Jake watched her reassessing her past with the man.

"How well did Bryan Mortimer get along with Jerome Wexler?" he asked.

"They were thick as thieves," she said. Her voice was quieter and had lost some of its energy. "Seemed like they'd known each other for years."

"And what was Bryan like?"

Ruby studied him for a moment. "Well, I could tell you a lie, but I don't ever plan to work with him again, so I guess it doesn't matter. He was an absolute nightmare. We were lucky we finished the shoot only a week overdue. He was late and erratic. I thought most the time he was on some kind of drug, probably cocaine, which was always a favorite in town, but he was so weird. He behaved like a bratty child."

"And the producers and executives allowed that to happen?" Jake asked.

"It was part of his auteur image," she said. "These male directors think they can behave atrociously and get away with it. It's their way of asserting dominance and testing the boundaries. If their box office to bullshit ratio is in line, they get away with it. But their box office must be pretty high for that. Anyway, look at him now."

"Failing up worked for him, did it?" Jake asked.

"Did it ever," Ruby said and leaned in, speaking low. "I'm still convinced someone else directed all his films. Likely some really talented editor somewhere. I don't believe that work is coming out of that man. He completely shat on everything and everyone from start to finish on that that film. I've never seen anything like it."

"And how was he with women?" Jake asked.

"There are always young women hanging around Bryan because he's a director. It was no different then. But the producers were like that, too. It was a real boy's club back then, granted not much has changed," Ruby said with a scowl.

"Do you have any idea where Jerome Wexler is now?" he asked.

"No and that's probably a good thing," Ruby said. "Last time I saw him was in 1995. I'd almost forgotten about him until you called me."

"Were there any ever rumors of parties where men were having sex with young girls under the influence?" he asked.

Ruby's laugh came out as harsh and strangled. "Are you kidding me? That happens almost every night in this goddamn town."

"If this industry is so toxic to women, why have you stayed in it so long?" Jake asked.

"Because it's my dream," Ruby said simply as she shrugged. "Where else am I gonna go?"

Jake nodded in understanding and stood to go.

"Thank you so much for meeting with me," Jake said.

"May I ask a favor of you, Mr. FBI Profiler?"

Jake smiled. "Sure."

"If you ever decide to write, call me first please?" She looked almost childlike as she smiled sweetly. "Because I got some real good stories that could use some FBI profiling clout behind them."

She was dead serious, Jake thought. "I'm not planning on joining your ranks yet, thank you though," he said.

"All right," she said as she stood up. "Can I ask you another favor?"

"Shoot," Jake said.

"Find that piece of shit Jerome Wexler and make him pay."

Jake nodded solemnly.

"I will, Ruby. If he's out there, I'll find him," he said, and she led him to the front door. "

"Remember, when you're ready for a career change, you call me first. You promised," she said.

"My first call," Jake promised and shook her hand.

As Jake headed back to his car, he thought maybe not everyone in Hollywood was a jaded narcissist. She'd given him another name to research.

Unfortunately, Bryan Mortimer was one of the biggest directors in the world. To say he was the elite of the elite in Hollywood was not giving the guy his due. And he was a longtime associate of Jerome Wexler's?

Jake doubted he'd even be able to speak to Bryan Mortimer. He wouldn't care if he was once an FBI profiler. Also, what if he knew about or was part of what Jerome Wexler was producing at that camp in Oregon? That would be a career killer for Mortimer and his people would never allow Jake near him.

He took the last steps down fast and breathed in the salty air as he got to his car. He needed a minute to think and being so close to the beach only reminded him of how much he missed it. Lauren. He pushed the thought of her in Oregon out of his mind and thought of her at the ocean's edge. Laughing.

He decided to take a walk along the Santa Monica boardwalk before he drove home. He needed to think, and he couldn't keep the ocean away forever.

The implications of what Ruby had told him clicked in his mind as he walked and breathed in the ocean breeze. Jerome Wexler surrounded himself with wealth and important people. As did Bryan Mortimer. Clearly two narcissists. Also, the rich inevitably stuck with their own kind. Safety in numbers.

If Harri had stumbled onto an organization of rich and powerful men abusing young girls, they would have enough money and influence to throw at any investigation that came their way. Narcissists always believed they were above the law.

He took out his phone to call Harri, but hesitated. He decided he would keep walking just a bit longer. They'd been picking up steam since returning from Oregon and it felt right. He was ecstatic enough to think about moving forward, even moving in.

Jake wanted to have a life and even though they still hadn't found Lauren's killer, they were working together. He didn't like going back and forth between their houses and wished he could see her every morning.

After this case was over, he would bring it up and see what she thought. When she'd told him she'd been followed, fear and rage came over him. He couldn't lose Harri, too. Not when they'd just discovered each other again.

Jake knew she could protect herself, probably better than he could protect her. It would make him sleep better at night knowing she was next to him, by his side. Heart to heart.

DAY 4

Harri inhaled the rose scented air deeply as she walked toward Roxanne's gate. The light dappled and gently shifted with the breeze in the trees above her.

Harri breathed the fragrance of the roses in and tried to get the smell of death and cigarettes to fade from memory. She'd berated herself all the way over to Roxanne's about Stephen and how she'd failed to protect him. She hoped Roxanne would allow the LAPD to protect her.

Harri stepped into the backyard and up to the front door of the guest house. Roxanne was already there waiting for her. Harri could see by the woman's blotched cheeks and watery eyes that she'd been crying.

"Thank you for meeting with me again, Roxanne," Harri said.

"I knew you'd be back, but I'm going to disappoint you again."

Harri stepped inside and Roxanne gestured to the same chair she'd sat in the night she'd first seen her.

Roxanne perched on the end of the couch, her body tense.

"Will you please come forward with your allegations and name the person who abused you?" Harri asked bluntly.

"I can't do that," Roxanne said

"We can protect you," Harry said.

"Like you protected Stephen Ladner?" Roxanne asked bitterly.

The news had already gotten out.

"He refused to help me and didn't trust me," Harri explained. "He never gave me names or his article. I believe he was double dealing in some way."

"And he ended up dead," Roxanne shook her head. "Don't you get it? These people are for real and I don't want to be dead, either."

"Roxanne, if you come forward and name them, you'll be a protected witness. Right now, you're an anonymous woman living in Los Angeles," Harri said. She was laying it on a little thick, but Roxanne's statement was all she had without Stephen Ladner's research.

"I'll never work again," Roxanne said. "You don't know what it was like. I had to crawl back from the brink of nothing. I had to fight my way back and what have I got? Voice overs and student films? I can't show my face in town as it is. They would destroy me."

"Roxanne, you're a victim" Harri said. "Please, let me help you."

"I am not a victim," Roxanne shook her head. "I have to acknowledge and be responsible for my own actions."

Harri recognized the words that must have come from Roxanne's therapist.

"I got things out of it, too," Roxanne continued. "That will all be brought up if this all gets out. I can't get dragged through the mud like Lydia was." Roxanne was talking fast again, like the night before."

"Lydia?" Harri asked.

"Lydia Marcos. She filed her complaint and it spread like wildfire all over town. And she never worked again. They said she was crazy, a troublemaker, a liar, and she got blacklisted. She never worked again. I can't do that. I can't."

"Where can I find Lydia Marcos?" Harri asked.

"I don't know," Roxanne mumbled. "I haven't seen her. I don't know."

"Roxanne," Harri's voice was sharp to get her attention. "Where can I find Lydia Marcos?"

"I, all I have is an old number," Roxanne said meekly. "The one I gave Stephen Ladner. Did he call her?"

"He might have," Harri said.

"If I give you her number will you leave me alone?"

"Roxanne, you know you're in danger," Harri said.

"Not if I keep my mouth shut," Roxanne said.

"And what if they think you've already talked?" Harri hated scaring Roxanne, but it seemed like the only thing that worked.

"What kind of things did you get out of your assault?" Harri asked.

"I had a career because of the man I had sex with," Roxanne said in an exhausted voice. "He introduced me to a producer who gave me my first job. I should have never been there. I knew better, but I was. And then I got something from it. So, if I went and told on him then people would say why are you telling on him five years later? You never spoke up before. You never went to the police. You accepted the parts you got because of it. You wanted it. I know #metoo has shifted things around, but the women are still judged. Still blamed."

"Roxanne," Harri said carefully. "All of that is possible, but what if precisely because of the movement that's happening right now your story is ripe for the telling? What if people understood that you didn't choose to have sex with him? He assaulted you. He abused his power to coerce you to do things you didn't want to do. That's what #metoo is about."

"That happens in Hollywood every day. We choose to work in this industry, don't we?" Roxanne countered.

"Roxanne, I want to help you. I want to protect you. But you have to go on record with everything."

"I'm not telling you a damn thing."

"Then give me Lydia's number at least," Harri asked.

Roxanne texted her the phone number.

"Thank you," Harri said. "I'm putting a protective detail on your place for the next few days."

"No!" Roxanne shouted. "I don't need that. If you do that, they'll think I did talk. And I haven't. I'm safe if I don't say anything."

"Really, Roxanne? You think you're safe?" Harri asked. "Have you been approached by any strangers?? Have you seen any strange cars in the vicinity?"

"You're scaring me," Roxanne said.

"Good, because you should be afraid. Stephen Ladner is dead. Sophie Lambert is dead. There are two girls who are still missing. And you have information that could tie it all together. Are you afraid yet, Roxanne?"

"I'm not telling you anything," Roxanne hissed. "I'm not going on record, so I don't need protection."

Harri was quiet, giving Roxanne room to calm down.

"You won't even see the uniforms there," Harri said.

"What will my neighbors think?" Roxanne asked. "If

they check on me and see cops, they'll think I talked to you."

Roxanne had tears in her eyes again. Something was off and Harri couldn't quite but her finger on it.

"Roxanne, what is this really about?" she asked.

"I was coerced, but I did things. Shameful, gross things. I don't want that stuff coming out," she said.

"What kind of things?" Harri asked, remembering what Stephen Ladner said about how the organization used shame against its victims.

"I don't really want to talk about it."

"Are you getting help?" Harri asked.

"I have a therapist, if I can keep her. I still have to book more jobs this year so I can qualify for SAG insurance."

"Roxanne, I'm going to do everything I can to get to the bottom of this organization, whether you help me or not. I want to find the people who did this to you and make them pay."

"Good luck with that, Detective Harper," Roxanne said bitterly. "If you do it, it will be a miracle."

The interview was over and Harri stood up to go. Roxanne had given her another contact to track down. Hopefully, that would lead to more. As Harri headed for the door, she took one last look at Roxanne. She looked like a child, folded up as small as she could make herself on the couch. Harri decided she would order the drive-bys for the next few days, regardless of what Roxanne's wishes were.

She wouldn't have another death on her conscience. Not if she could help it.

· · ·

When she got back into her car, she looked down at her phone. An email notification sat blinking on her screen. It showed an email from Stephen Ladner. She clicked it open.

The email was sent yesterday afternoon and had no subject. In the body of the email was one word.

Rosebud.

DAY 4

Debi Mills woke up to another splitting headache.

She had no idea how long she'd been out for, but she could tell by the light outside it was getting to be nighttime.

She moved her battered body off the bed and found herself naked. Bruises dotted her skin all over her breasts, arms, and thighs. Her thighs looked the worst.

She staggered over to the window to try to open it like before, but it was locked. She balled her hands up into fists and smashed them against the windowpane, hoping the force of the blows would shatter the glass.

It was useless. The window stayed in one piece while her fists throbbed in pain. More pain to deal with, she thought. She shuffled back to the bed and saw the tray of food next to the door. She lifted the top cover and found a plate of fried chicken, French fries, coleslaw, and a thermos of ice water. Seeing the ice water made her realize how incredibly thirsty she was. She gulped it down too fast and coughed hard, straining her neck. Would the pain ever stop?

She waited for the water to settle in her empty stomach before grabbing a chicken leg and stuffing it into her mouth. Debi stayed with her back against the door, hoping the camera wouldn't catch her desperate eating. After the chicken leg, came the French fries, surprisingly still warm, then the coleslaw. She ate with her hands as there were no utensils, but there were paper napkins.

Her stomach growled. She went from being famished to feeling ill. Again. She'd eaten too fast and drank too much water and everything was swishing around. She didn't want to puke up her only sustenance.

Debi stumbled back to the bed and sat there trying to get her digestive system under control while swallowing down bile.

What had they done to her that she couldn't even keep food down? A sudden wave of dizziness washed over, and she vomited all over her hands and the carpeted floor.

Gross, she thought. At least, she'd missed the bed.

Debi hobbled over to the small bathroom that had a sink and a toilet and washed the vomit off her hands. She grabbed one of the towels and did her best to clean up the vomit next to the bed so she wouldn't have to smell it.

A strange feeling crept over her body, causing her vision to swim and her legs to feel weak. She crumpled to the floor again. The walls looked like they were falling on top of her head. She lifted her hands up to protect herself, but nothing hit her. Laying on the floor, next to the partially cleaned-up vomit, Debi realized what had just happened.

The food or the water had been drugged. She'd fallen for it again. Why had she eaten? Why did she drink the water when could have gotten some from the tap?

They were coming in when she was passed out and doing things to her while she was out. Her last thought before she lost consciousness again was how long she could survive only drinking water.

Her world turned black.

When Debi awoke, she was back in the narrow bed. Her hair had been washed because and smelled of shampoo. Her body had been scrubbed clean, too. She was wearing a soft, plush robe and nothing else. It felt so good against her skin and she lay there, curled up in a ball, stroking the sleeve.

Next to her lay a skimpy dress and a black lace bra and panties set. She didn't want to put the clothes on, but what choice did she have? What would they do to her if she refused?

Debi lay on her side on the bed in her prison. Flashes of dark rooms, people laughing, the smell of alcohol and marijuana filled her senses. Had they taken her out of this room already? She tried to remember, but the little movie clips in her mind slipped away.

If her vomit had prevented her from ingesting all the drugs they'd given her, then maybe she could keep it together to make a run for it. Getting out of this room had been her only goal. Now, with her growing aware-ness of the situation she was in, she came up with a new plan. A plan that involved staying coherent.

If they let her out of this room, then that changed everything. She wouldn't drink or eat anything else they gave her. Water was important, though. She had fresh water coming out of the sink. How could she pretend she was eating and drinking what they gave her? Could she hide it and flush it down the toilet?

Now that Debi could think clearly, her mind raced to find solutions. She would pretend to eat and drink what they gave her if she was ever put back in the prison. Maybe that wouldn't happen, though.

She would put on the clothes. They wanted to dress her up for something, but what? Was she leaving the room or was someone coming in? No, whoever they were dressing her up for wasn't coming to this disgusting prison cell, she thought.

Tonight, would be the night she'd run for it. They first had to come and get her out of the room. With less drugs in her system, she'd finally have a chance to escape. Bolstered by hope, she pulled on the sexy panties. She kept the robe on for another minute. It reminded her of the robe she had at home.

Debi would make it back home. It was a promise she would keep to herself.

29

DAY 4 – EARLY EVENING

Harri opted to call Lydia Marcos to make sure she would be home for the meeting. Lydia invited her to come immediately and gave her an address far up in the Hollywood Hills above Bel Air on Mulholland Drive.

For someone who lost their entire Hollywood career, Lydia Marcos' address spoke of wealth and privilege, not a ruined life. Harri was encouraged by that.

Guilt weighed heavily on Harri as she replayed the interview she'd had with Roxanne in her mind. Had she pushed her too hard? She'd been lucky Roxanne had given her Lydia's number. She could have just as easily kicked her out of her home.

Whatever Roxanne had done was eating her up. Like a sick ripple effect, the repercussions reverberating over the years of this organization's twisted actions echoed all over the city in the damage it did to its victims. Harri wanted justice for all each one of them.

She drove up Laurel Canyon all the way to the crest

of the hill and turned left onto Mulholland Drive. The drive was a famous street in Los Angeles that ran all the way to the ocean. It was mostly a twisty two-lane road with multiple million-dollar homes flanking either side.

It was also the road where people regularly got into accidents due to speeding around curves while staring out into the lush beauty of the Los Angeles Basin with wonder. The whole city could be seen from that vantage point.

A screeching of tires made her look in her rearview mirror. She frowned when she saw a black sports car speeding toward her at breakneck speed. Harri was going around a sharp curve with no shoulder. She couldn't get out of the car's way.

She flashed her brake light several times. If the car went that fast around the curve, it would definitely hit her. Harri drove well enough, but she wasn't skilled at evasive driving and there was nowhere to go. If she went into the opposite lane to avoid him, she could be in a head-on collision, as there was no visibility to oncoming traffic.

The sports car revved its engine behind her. She looked back in the mirror and it was right on her tail.

Harri flashed her brake lights again.

The sports car hit her hard.

Harri's car lurched forward and she almost lost her grip on the steering wheel.

And there was another curve coming up. She sped up to get some space between her and the sports car.

It sped up, too and hit her again, even harder this time. Her sweaty palms gripped the wheel as if her life depended on it because it did. Harri scanned the road for any sign of a shoulder.

There was no room between the road and rocky incline to her right.

Harri gunned the engine even more. The speed limit here was only forty miles an hour and rightly so with the blind curves coming every half a mile. She was now going well past that.

The black sports car gave chase.

Crap. She couldn't go any faster.

Harri was in a standard black police cruiser. If it hit the cruiser on the side instead of behind, it would likely receive more damage than the cruiser. Harri gently pressed on the brake. The black car didn't and hit her again.

Harri scanned for any driveways she could use to get out of this car's way. Seeing a clearing up ahead, Harri let the wheel drift to her right while also slowing down.

The black sports car's engine whined as the curve forced him to brake as well. Harri took that as her opportunity.

She twisted the steering wheel hard to the right as she jammed the breaks. She held on as tightly as she could, praying she wouldn't spin out. Her tires held and her car slowed way down, hitting grass and gravel on the lawn of a massive mansion.

The black sports car whizzed by her, unable to brake as hard and disappeared around the car. With Harri's adrenaline messing with her focus, she didn't catch his plate.

Panic washed over her as her system went into total fight or flight. Harri placed her forehead on the steering wheel and let the stress wrack her body as she breathed deeply.

Someone had tried to run her off the road. There was no doubt that this time, it wasn't a warning. If this yard hadn't come up when it had, she would be smashed into a dirt wall.

Harri focused on her breathing until the trembling throughout her body began to fade. She knew what was happening and worked to ride it out. It wasn't every day someone tried to kill you, she thought.

30

DAY 4 – EARLY EVENING

Harri sat in her car working through the aftereffects of being run off the road for close to an hour.

In that time, she'd called Lydia Marcos to make sure she was still home and would speak to her. Harri preferred to arrive unannounced so witnesses couldn't prepare their statements ahead of time. With her near-death experience, Harri decided to call again to recon-firm she would be available.

Roxanne's description of Lydia's potentially fragile mental state had given her pause. She didn't want to trigger her as she had with Roxanne.

To Harri's surprise, Lydia told her to come right over. The mansion was only ten minutes away from where the accident happened. Harri parked the cruiser behind a Mercedes. She walked behind and looked at the damage. She wanted to laugh, but held it in. There were some dings and scratches, but no real damage. Did a little black sports car really think it could take an LAPD cruiser? She shook her head and smiled. Harri really needed that change in mood.

She was walking up the drive when the door opened. A slim woman with silvery white hair emerged from the shadows of the doorway and smiled.

"You must be Detective Harper," she said. "Welcome."

"I am and thank you for giving me your time," Harri said and joined her at the door.

"You are too good-looking to be a cop," Lydia said with a friendly smile.

Harri waved her comment off. "Detective actually."

"My bad, sorry. It's impressive that you're a detective," Lydia said. "And a detective who investigates murders? You must have seen some things."

She led Harri through a foyer that was open to the third floor. Paintings of various sized covered the wall all the way to the top. Harri glanced around. Everything was elegant and inviting. Harri knew it had to have been designed by an interior decorator. Harri had been in multi-millionaire's homes before, but nothing as grand as this.

"I know what you're thinking 'how did a washed-up actress land digs like these'. Am I right?"

"Your artwork is impressive," Harri said.

"I married well," Lydia said as she led Harri through what might be the living room, or parlor, or? Harri wasn't sure. It was big, elegant, with a fireplace. "My husband works in finance."

"Smart husband," Harri said.

"It also helps that I came from money," Lydia said with a smile.

Harri liked the no-nonsense attitude of this woman. She didn't seem unstable as Roxanne indicated. Lydia had a striking square face, with full lips, and pale blue eyes. And that silvery white blonde hair.

"Your hair, such a unique color," Harri said.

"It's gray," Lydia smiled. "I stopped coloring it and went natural. I got lucky it's turned out such a nice shade."

"Gray? You can't be older than thirty?" Harri asked.

"I'm thirty-two. Premature gray runs in my family. I already had gray hairs as a teenager."

"What color was it before?" Harri asked.

"A pale blonde, but I like this better. I was ready for a change," she said and led Harri into the kitchen. Harri glanced around and took in the space. It was simple, clean, and classic with white cabinetry reminiscent of a country home and top-of-the-line appliances. The walls were a pale yellow and the floor was black-and-white checkered pattern of marble. The diamond-paned windows overlooked the greenery of what Harri guessed was a backyard as lush as a home like this demanded.

Lydia approached a central island where a pitcher of pink lemonade, a crystal bucket of ice, and two glasses had been set.

"Would you like some lemonade? I was craving something sweet, but sour" Lydia explained as she sat on one of the stools and grabbed a glass.

"I would love some," Harri said as she sat next to her.

Lydia poured her a glass and handed it to her, then sighed lightly. "So, what do you want to know?"

"Why didn't your complaint go public?" Harri asked. "When I did a search on you nothing came up."

"My husband," Lydia said simply. "He was my boyfriend at the time and wanted to protect me. He deals with vicious people all the time in the work that he does, and he didn't think the police could do a damn thing for me."

Harri was disappointed to hear that.

"What exactly does her husband do?" Harri asked.

"He runs a fund, to put it simply. He deals with all kinds, and every day he has to navigate deals with people who...like to walk on the shady side of the street, if you understand my meaning."

Harri nodded. She didn't know much about the world of finance, but she could guess. That's the world Jerome Wexler thrived in, after all.

"So, I chose to go to HR instead." Lydia said. "Thinking that something could be done quietly in the system. How naïve was I? The studios don't publicize those kinds of complaints and I'd chosen the wrong people to bring it to."

Harri raised an eyebrow. "Okay backup, what were you doing when this happened?" Harri asked, retrieving her notebook out of her bag.

"I had a supporting role in a feature film and was shooting on one of the studio lots. It was a pretty big studio picture. A good hundred million and they had a top-of-the-line director. Have you ever heard of Bryan Mortimer?" Lydia asked.

"Yes, I've heard of him," Harri said. "He's done some of the biggest films in the last decade?"

"Exactly. You say his name and people in the business start tossing out terms like genius and auteur," Lydia said as she rolled her eyes and took a sip.

"Was your HR complaint against Bryan Mortimer?"

"It was," she said. "He's the worst of them all."

Harri looked up sharply. "What do you mean the worst of them all?" she asked.

"If you've spoken to Roxanne, you already know the

basic story," Lydia said.Harri nodded. "I need to hear about your experience," Harri said. "I realize this will be difficult, but in order to see the differences and similarities in your stories, I have to get first-person accounts. You were also a victim?"

"I was worse than a victim," Lydia said carefully.

Harri had an idea of what she was getting at.

"What is worse than a victim?" Harri asked.

"Being both victim and perpetrator," Lydia said.

"Explain this to me because I don't understand how.".″

"I had auditioned and booked my second supporting part on a feature film," Lydia began. "Yay me. I was only seventeen and I was ecstatic to be working with a big director like Bryan. He was friendly and professional, and I thought he was treating me like a grown up. At first, I mean. That was during rehearsals and for the first days of shooting and then things got weird."

Harri nodded, staying silent and jotting down the story.

"One of our days ran really late and I was in one of the last scenes on the schedule. We finished the scene and I went back to the trailer to pack up to go home. One of the production assistants knocked on my door and said Bryan wanted to see me before I left.

"Is this kind of thing normal on film sets?" Harri asked.

"It's normal when it's not Bryan Mortimer," Lydia said. "He was a famous director. I had two lines in the scene, eight lines in the entire film. I was pretty much a nobody. He had no reason to need to speak to me," she said, shaking her head. "It was only my second feature film and I thought I'd made it," she said and laughed.

Her composure had changed as had the tone of the

laugh. Harri noted an air of sadness had entered their conversation. Harri fought the urge to take Lydia's hand and comfort her.

"Then what happened?" Harri asked.

Lydia took another sip of lemonade and hesitated a moment before continuing. "So, I get to his trailer and he's there all by himself. He comes at me telling me how good I was and how he wishes my part was bigger. He's thinking of having the screenwriter beef up my part. I was such a fool. I was surprised, but I believed him, thinking I was some sort of hot shit. He offered me a drink to celebrate my new breakout role. Of course, I took the drink."

"And then?"

Lydia paused again and Harri waited patiently until she spoke again.

"And then I woke up in a prison."

Harri waited again.

"It was a disgusting little room with a window and a door. The door was locked, the window opaque glass, but I could see bars were on the outside. There was a toilet and a sink."

Harri waited for Lydia to continue.

"My lady bits were on fire and I saw blood on the sheets of the bed," Lydia said, her voice a soft monotone.

"He sexually assaulted you?" Harri asked.

"I was sexually assaulted, yes. I don't know by who."

"Bryan Mortimer imprisoned you?"

Lydia nodded. "For what I found out was two days. He let me out and told me the screenwriter had finished the new scenes and I was now one of the main bad guys. He gave me some bullshit story of wanting to see how I would react if I was imprisoned. For the film, of course. Method acting."

"What about the sexual assault?"

"I had absolutely no memory of how that happened. It had to be pretty rough sex because I was in so much pain and the bleeding wouldn't stop. When I went to my gynecologist, she told me I had a ton of vaginal tearing. She asked me to chill on the rough sex. I was so embarrassed."

"You assumed it was him, though?" Harri asked, keeping her voice gentle.

"Yes," Lydia said. "I'd had that drink with him in his trailer. Alone. Then I wake up at his compound with no memory of anything that happened. I'm in pain and bleeding down there. Then he just gives me the part of a lifetime in a Bryan Mortimer film. I was nineteen and had no idea what the hell was happening. I'd heard of method acting and the lengths some actors went to get into character. I was just totally confused."

"And how long ago was this," Harri asked.

"About twelve years ago," she said.

"And when did you file the complaint with HR?" Harri asked.

"A year later. So that would have been 2007."

"Why HR?"

"That's where I made my biggest mistake and became a perpetrator. I finished that film and it did great at the box office. My agent called me about another Bryan Mortimer film. One I didn't have to audition for. Bryan thought I was perfect for the part."

A tear formed in the corner of Lydia's eye and she blinked it away. She gulped down her glass of lemonade as Harri stayed silent, waiting for her to compose herself. It took some moments for her to speak again.

"In my mind, I had officially made it. I didn't have to audition? That was hitting the big time. Then I received a call from his producer, Michael Tisland. Bryan wanted to personally invite me and my friends, Lola and Anna, to a party he was having that night. He urged me to go. For my career."

Harri stopped writing and looked up. Lydia took a deep breath and smoothed her hair. Lydia avoided making eye contact.

"Looking back, I knew what he was telling me. If I wanted the part, I needed to show up with my two best girlfriends. I didn't even question how he knew we were all friends. I talked myself into going with them. I wanted that part. I wanted this all to be in some way normal."

"So, you three went to the party?"

"Yes, and Bryan was a perfect gentleman. He introduced us to some important people. Lola and Anna hadn't gotten any big credits yet and were so thankful that I'd included them," Lydia said, choking out the last part.

"At some point in the night, I lost track of the both of them. I searched through his massive estate and couldn't find either of them. Lots of industry people were there and I convinced myself they must have met some guys and went off to party with them. I convinced myself that my experience with Bryan was only a one-off weird method acting thing," she said.

"Did you find them?"

"No." Lydia closed her eyes and shook her head. She opened them again and pursed her lips. "I went home. I didn't really sleep that night. Kept calling Lola's cell phone. Anna didn't have one. Neither of them picked up. I finally saw Lola two days later.

"And she was okay?" Harri asked.

"She didn't want to let me into her apartment. She

had a black eye. I got her to let me in and she told me she'd been drugged and assaulted by two men at the party. We still had no idea where Anna was."

"Did you find Anna?"

"She turned up a week later. Wouldn't talk to me or Lola. She went back home to Florida, like two days later."

"Did you go to the police?" Harri asked.

"What would I have gone to them with?" Lydia asked. "Anna was gone. Lola wouldn't go with me. I had no idea what had really happened. That's when my husband explained the only way to get leverage over Bryan Mortimer would be through the studio. They had a financial stake and could be held liable for his actions, so they were the gateway to stopping whatever it was he was doing."

"Why didn't your husband think the police would be able to do anything?"

Lydia sighed. "Because they didn't do a damn thing when he went to them about what his first boss was doing. All they did was tell his boss he had a rat on his ship."

Harri nodded. Money had spoken and Lydia's husband had been burned. Understandably, he wanted to protect her.

"So, I went to HR, thinking I could do something while not going public. I wanted to be an actor. I was still wrapped up in the dream. I had a big part written for me. The guilt of what I'd done to Lola and Anna sent me spiraling into a deep depression. Remember I was only twenty then. It's not an excuse. I should have known. I chose my career and served up my friends to be raped." She let out a guttural, bitter laugh. "Joke was on me though."

"HR didn't do anything about it?" Harri asked.

"HR at the studio turned out to be neither human, nor resourceful. It's there to protect the company, not the employees."

"Who did you speak to in HR?"

"A man named William Valance."

"Anyone else?"

"He was my only contact before everything exploded. I had a lawyer question me, my motives. He accused me of fabricating a story to get back at Bryan. It had come out that the part was pulled from me and given to another actor. The studio chalked my story up to sour grapes over being passed over for a role. I never went to the police when it happened. By that time, nearly a year had passed since the incident. It was hearsay. He said/she said. You get the picture."

"Do you remember the lawyer's name?"

"No."

"Did you go to the police then?" Harri asked.

"No," Lydia smiled ruefully. "By then I was self-medicating to deal with my depression. The guilt and the shame and feelings of defeat had pushed me over the edge in a dark place of worthlessness. I wanted to kill myself over what happened to Lola and Anna. My agent dropped me. Every day a new rumor of mental illness was making the rounds," Lydia said as she wiped away a forming tear with the back of her hand.

"I'm so sorry," Harri said.

"I couldn't reconcile what I'd done to my friends. Or to myself. And for what? A part in a film. I had destroyed two lives, just to get more lines. The PTSD of it all reared its head, too. My biggest acting role was given to me in payment for my silence about being held prisoner and raped. What kind of person did that make me?"

"It wasn't your fault."

"I made a choice about Lola and Anna," Lydia said. "My husband stood up for me. He lost his job as a production accountant too, for trying to speak out. I don't know why he kept choosing me, but he did. We got married and decided to just leave the industry entirely. Then their leverage over us evaporated. The best decision we ever made."

"And then?"

"And then," Lydia finally smiled a real smile. "I cleaned up and went into therapy. We bought this place and made a new life. It was all about recovery and reconciling with my past. Until I met Roxanne."

"Tell me about that." Harri said.

"I was at a party, a benefit for climate change and overheard two actresses speaking about Bryan Mortimer. One of the them was Roxanne Miles."

"You exchanged stories?" Harri asked.

"Yes, and I found out his hobby had grown into a full-blown organization helping him facilitate all kinds of assaults. All over town at different parties with a whole crew of men getting off on young girls. I've talked to at least ten actresses in the last five years that were assaulted at one of these parties, but they're afraid to come forward because of what happened to me. I voluntarily left the business and I had my own money and my husband who believed me and supported me in every way. Mortimer and his people tried to destroy me with their lies and manipulations, but I was able to walk away. None of these other girls had the options I had. Every day I'm so thankful I had the strength and the money to just walk away. And for my husband."

"What about the #metoo movement?" Harri asked.

"One man is one thing, detective," Lydia said. "A

group of enormously powerful men? What young girl can defend herself against them? I'm used as an example of what happens when a woman speaks out. Not to mention they weaponise shame. The girls I spoke to also brought their friends to parties. The shame is key to keeping it under wraps. It's the secret ingredient. They manipulate these girls into becoming both victims and perpetrators, like I was. It's an extreme form of cognitive dissonance. Our brains can't handle the implications of those actions. Especially when the girls get some kind of reward as payment for their betrayal."

"Did you ever meet a Georgie Shipwell?" Harri asked.

"No."

"She's the daughter of Glenn Shipwell."

"The western actor from the seventies?"

"Yes, that one."

"No, our paths never crossed. Why?" Lydia asked.

"She's apparently Bryan Mortimer's right-hand woman. Roxanne mentioned she'd groomed her. I'm having an incredibly hard time finding her. She's not in the DMV database. Can't find her online. She has no record."

"Famous people live in a different world than you and I. It sounds like her name is her stage name and not her real name. She might have chosen it to match more closely to her father's name for the access it would grant. You need to know her real name to find all the information you're looking for," Lydia explained.

Harri put her pen down. "Is Hollywood completely based in fiction?"

"Yes," Lydia said.

The two women sat in the sunny warmth of the beautiful, cottage-white kitchen and rested in their thoughts. After several moments Harri turned to Lydia.

"Thank you for telling me your story," Harri said. "I know it must have been difficult."

Lydia shook her head. "It's not difficult. It's healing to tell it. And it's necessary. People need to know. I told you not for myself, but for all the other victims out there. For Lola and Anna."

Would any of these girls be willing to talk?"

"I've called six of them and they agreed to speak with you." Lydia turned and grabbed a purse at her feet and pulled out a sheet of paper with the information.

"All the stories are similar," Lydia remarked. "I've also listed their addresses. I'm hoping you'll move quickly on this?"

"You have been the first woman to give us his name," Harri nodded. "No one else would name who'd assaulted them."

"They can't do anything to me anymore," Lydia said. "I have funding. I have lawyers. And I have friends. The girls I've spoken to don't have that."

"Thank you for your bravery," Harri said. "Do you have a security team?"

"Oh yes, detective." Lydia smiled. "Like I said, they can't do anything to me anymore."

"Well, tell them to be vigilant. When this comes out, I'm afraid Bryan Mortimer might come for you."

"Honestly, detective, I wish he would. I've been fantasizing about that for years. If that disgusting piece of shit comes anywhere near me, I'll kill him," Lydia stated flatly.

And Harri believed her.

31

DAY 4 – EVENING

"We have a name," said Harri.

She'd called Tom the moment she got back into her car. She pulled out of Lydia's driveway and drove to an overlook nearby. She parked the car and watched the sun go down over the LA Basin. It was magical. She needed the calmness right now.

"Stop shouting," Tom said. "I can hear you. Anyone we've come across in the investigation so far?"

"You will not believe who it is," Harri said.

"Public figure?" asked Tom.

"Affirmative," Harri said with a smile, enjoying the game.

"Producer?"

"No."

"Studio Head?"

"Keep guessing."

"Actor?"

"No."

"Aw, shit. I don't know. Just tell me."

"Bryan Mortimer."

"No."

"Yes!" Harri shouted.

"Oh, this is gonna be a media circus," Tom said. "Three rings. With elephants. Your witness specifically said he sexually assaulted her?"

"Not exactly," Harri said. "He held her prisoner, though. And she was raped in captivity. This happened about twelve years ago on her second movie. He was the director. She also said he drugged her, so she didn't remember much of it."

"Did she report it to the police?" Tom asked. "I can dig up the original."

"She reported it to HR at the studio where the film was being shot. Unfortunately, it was almost a year later after she discovered some of her actor friends had been assaulted at one of his parties. The studio quashed the allegation and blackballed her. She never went to the police."

"The girls bring their friends to be abused?" Tom asked.

Harri wasn't sure if it was incredulity or disgust she heard in his voice. Probably both, she thought as she was the sun dip below the horizon and the sky turn purple. Harri sighed. Her nerves were shot from the conversations she'd had with Roxanne and Lydia and her harrowing encounter with the black sports car. Still needed to report the accident, she thought.

"That's how this has been kept silent for all these years," Harri said. "They traffic in shame."

"This is a tangle, Harri." Tom said. "One of the world's most famous directors drugging and raping underage actresses, a studio that knew about it and did nothing. This implicates so many people. The net's getting pretty big."

"Lydia was nineteen at the time, so technically not underage," Harri said.

"Still. Most of his other victims were."

Harri needed to tell Tom about the black sports car. She worried he'd force her back to the office. She had to go talk to the women on the list Lydia gave her. What if they were already being intimidated not to speak with her?

"I forgot to mention," she said casually. "Someone tried to kill me on the way to Lydia's."

There was silence on the other end of the line before Tom exploded. "What! What the hell are telling me, Harri?"

"A black sports car tried to run me off the road. He hit my back bumper at a high speed, on a curve on Mulholland. I think he was trying to make me spin out and go over the edge."

"Are you all right?" Tom asked. "Can you drive?"

"This car's a tank. I barely saw any scratches on the bumper. And yes, I'm fine."

"Did you get the plate?"

"No," Harri said. "I didn't get the make or model, either. It was black and low to the ground. A Porsche maybe?" Harri wasn't great at identifying European sports cars. "It happened so fast and I was on a super curvy part of Mulholland."

"That entire road is dangerous. Sure it wasn't just a joyrider?"

"Positive. He hit me deliberately three times and sped off after I skidded into someone's yard."

"You need to get checked out," Tom said.

"I'm fine."

"Harri." Tom warned.

"I will get checked out, Tom." She assured him. "First chance."

"Did she give you any other names?" Tom asked.

"She gave me the names of six women who have similar stories. But Tom. If what Lydia says it's true. There are hundreds of victims out there."

"I saw you put a protective detail on Roxanne Miles." Tom asked.

"After what happened with Stephen Ladner, I didn't want to take any chances."

"I'll be happy to tell Byrne we've definitely got information that makes this an RHD case," Tom remarked dryly.

"Are you still at Stephen Ladner's?"

"I finished up there, but CID is still on site. Grimley took the body and will get the autopsy in two days' time. She couldn't immediately rule out suicide, though. I had the crime techs try to create the pulley system used to hoist him up there. I can't see any way he'd be able to do that himself," Tom said.

"You and I know he didn't kill himself," Harri said.

"I agree. No way. What's your move now?"

"I'm going to start this list of victims. See if I can get more names. Lydia did give me the name of the man in HR she brought this to. William Valance."

"Call for backup if you need it. I'm worried they might come for you again. Have you seen your tail?"

"No."

"We have to assume they know you've uncovered Lydia Marcos."

"She seems to think they destroyed her credibility," Harri said. "She has a security team already, though. She's a rich lady."

"My kind of gal," Tom chortled.

"Oh, no. Happily married to what sounds like a wonderful man."

"All right. I'm on my way to see Byrne. Wish me luck. Wish I had my kryptonite with me."

"Aww, shucks, Tom," she said.

"Good luck with that list," Tom said, and they hung up.

Harri watched the sky darken into an indigo blue. The lights below twinkled in the November night sky.

She pulled the list of out her bag and scanned it to see if anyone jumped out at her. One of the addresses was in Los Feliz. She could get there in under an hour if the traffic gods were on her side. The rest of the addresses were deep in the valley. One was as far as Glendora. She'd be driving a lot to see them all.

She took one last look at the city below her and started up the car. Taking a deep breath, she pulled out onto Mulholland and headed east.

DAY 4 – EVENING

I t was only a twenty-minute drive to Los Feliz. When she pulled up, she was surprised to see it was a gated estate. From the sounds of laughter and loud music, Jennifer Randall was having a party. The estate was perched among a thicket of trees with the driveway going up steeply so she couldn't see what kind of house she going to. She had assumed all the girls on the list were former actresses. Jennifer must have come from money like Lydia or married well. She noticed the gate was locked and wondered how she could crash the party.

She decided to wait for some partygoers to come to the gate. Once the gate opened, she'd slip inside behind them. She found a good lookout area not too far away from the gate, turned off the engine and the lights, and made herself comfortable as she waited for her opportunity.

To her relief, she only had to wait about twenty minutes before a group of five men came walked by her, the smell of marijuana trailing behind them. They clicked the button on the security panel at the gate and she overheard one of them say "Sunset Boulevard."

The gate swung open.

Harri waited until the group was halfway up the driveway before locked the car and sprinted through the narrow gap between the gate and the wall. She'd almost missed her chance. She assumed there was a camera trained on the gate but hoped whoever was watching would mistake her as a party goer.

While she'd been waiting, she'd pulled her hair from the loose bun and mussed it up. She'd found an old red lipstick in the bottom of her purse and put that on. She'd taken off her white button-down shirt and wore only the white tank top underneath. With her black jeans, she looked almost like a woman going to a party.

She didn't look young, but she hoped Lydia was right about her good looks. Her heartbeat with excitement when she heard the group of men ahead use the password again. Could this be one of those secret Hollywood parties? And if so, why was one of Bryan Mortimer's victims listing it as her personal address.

Or had Lydia snuck in the address of the compound where she'd been held? Why wouldn't she have given the address outright? She hadn't held anything back. Thoughts cascaded in Harri's mind like a waterfall as she climbed the steep drive.

Once she reached level ground, she whistled under her breath. This estate was a compound. From her vantage point, she counted six buildings circling a kidney shaped pool. Tall fir trees surrounded the property for what she assumed would be privacy. It was the only property on this hill. The pool and outdoor spaces were filled with people, laughing and drinking.

The landscape was artfully lit up showcasing

different garden spaces. Some featured huge cacti and succulents, others featured roses and hedges. Twinkle lights were strung up between the buildings and some strands lit up the thicket of woods behind the buildings. The compound had a surreal quality about it: a mix of Salvador Dali and Dr. Seuss.

The partygoers seemed to be a mix of young women and older men. Nothing else. The young women were gorgeous. Perfect bodies, beautiful faces. The men, on the other hand, tended towards older, balding, with guts sticking out from their expensive suits. The median age of the men was fifty, Harri guessed. Harri could see some attractive men in their twenties scattered about. She assumed they must be actors or maybe some kind of crew.

The scene was like what Roxanne had described and Lydia alluded to. Harri smiled and shook her head. Lydia. What are you up to? No way Harri had simply stumbled into one of Bryan Mortimer's secret parties.

She chose one of the largest buildings to her right to go into. Harri knew what both Debi and Addy looked like. Would they be out and about? Required to service these men?

She walked into the largest building and saw it was equipped with a kitchen and a huge lofted living room with beams spanning the entire length. It had to be one of those heritage sites because the structure looked old and immaculately preserved. The furniture looked like curated antiques, and the paintings and art pieces were likely original.

Who was Jennifer Randall and did she really live here? Harri was beginning to think Lydia had landed her right into the middle of where she needed to be.

"Hey gorgeous," a voice came from behind her.

Harri turned to see a man in his fifties, with silver at his temples, wearing a buttoned-down shirt with his tie loosened, holding a whiskey in his hand.

"Hey baby. Pretty great party," Harri said in a light voice as she tossed her hair.

"Can I get you a drink?" he asked.

Harri assumed anything she touched would be tainted with drugs.

"I'm looking for the little girl's room," she said.

"I can take you there," he whispered in her ear. Harri fought the urge to punch him in the throat and instead shrank away from him and his whisky breath.

She dropped the sing-song voice. "I really need to use the bathroom. Do you know where it is?" she demanded in her best cop voice.

The man didn't like that. "Upstairs. The first door on the left."

She'd broken the spell and he turned away from her, muttering foul names at her under his breath.

She took the stairs two at a time to the second level. Wow. Climbing Jake's stairs were staring to pay off. She came to a hallway with four doors. Harri looked down at the living area and saw the man had found another woman to bother.

She opened the first door. It was indeed a bathroom. When she opened the second door, she saw two naked bodies in the middle of a bed having sex. Neither looked like Debi or Addison. She closed it again. Harri had no idea whether the sex was consensual or not.

Harri kept going. She opened a third door and found a pile of bodies engaged in various sex acts. Debi had copper hair and Addison had shoulder-length, light brown curls. Harri scanned for any signs of women resembling them and didn't find a redhead or curls among them.

She closed the door again. Harri was at the right place. Now, she just needed to find those girls before someone figured out she didn't belong there.

33

DAY 4 – EVENING

Debi must have passed out again because when she woke up it was dark in the room. She'd dressed in the clothes left for her and then waited. She'd sat on the bed and fought the increasing dizziness and strange euphoria that threatened to scatter her senses.

Her hunger was intense, and she'd taken a chance at nibbling on a piece of cake that came in plastic packaging with the rest of the food and the water left at the door. They must have laced the cake with the drugs too because she was feeling the effects without having tried anything else.

They weren't taking any chances, apparently, and had drugged every bit of food and water they had left her. The door finally opened to reveal a man standing in silhouette against the purplish light coming from the hallway. He looked familiar to Debi. Not someone she knew personally, but someone she'd seen somewhere. Someone she'd seen a lot.

Her vision was fuzzy, and she swiped at her eyes to make them less blurry.

"Hey girl," he crooned. "It's time to play."

Debi choked back a sob remembering that if she was able to get out of this room, she had a chance of escaping this horrible place.

She tried to stand on unsteady legs. The man came to her and put his arms around her waist to help her walk.

"You smell so good. I'm so glad you got cleaned up," he whispered in her ear.

Debi felt like a rag doll with her arms and legs flopping around as he pulled her out of her prison. How did any man find the shape she was in alluring?

"I have some friends I'd like you to meet," he said.

His words made her skin crawl.

"Friends?" she mumbled.

What were they planning to do to her?

As they made their way down the hall, she talked to herself.

Stay alert.

Keep yourself calm.

Keep walking so the movement will help your body digest the drugs quicker. He didn't know she hadn't eaten the food. She'd only pretended and hidden it in her robe, flushing each piece of chicken down the toilet.

She hoped her ruse worked.

Debi needed to fight through the grogginess and move her body. She relaxed into his grasp and let the man think she was more out of it than she really was. They expected her to be doped up, so she'd play the part.

When they finally got into more light, she looked at him and stifled a gasp.

She knew exactly who her captor was.

34

DAY 4 – EVENING

Harri Harper rushed down the stairs scanning faces of the young women that were still around the large living room chatting with men. When she didn't recognize any of the girls, she walked outside.

She had four more buildings to search, as well as the pool. Harri pulled her phone out of her pocket and texted Tom the address of the secret sex party she'd stumbled across, and that she was searching for Debi and Addison.

If you don't hear from me, send backup, she'd managed to write and send off as someone tapped her shoulder from behind.

Harri spun around, putting her phone into her back pocket to face a security guard.

"Stop right there." The man's voice was gruff and harsh.

"May I help you?" she asked in a calm and collected voice.

The man was wearing a wired headphone around his

ear and was dressed all in black. He had the ripped look of a guy who worked out way too much and enjoyed the fear his body instilled in other people.

"Cell phones aren't allowed at this party," he said.

"Oh, I must've missed where we were supposed to leave them," she said.

"Who invited you?" he demanded.

Harri paused and took a good look at the security guard as if to say, 'how dare you'. "I'm a production executive at one of the biggest studios in town. Bryan Mortimer invited me to come here tonight. You want to go and ask him about that?" she asked in a haughty tone, praying the use of Mortimer's name would make the guy back off.

The namedropping had the desired effect and the guy retreated, putting his hands up. "You know the security at these things then," he said.

Harri nodded.

"I still need your phone, though. I have a couple of bracelets on me to scan it in. On your way out, just go by the gatehouse and let them scan the bracelet and they'll give you back your phone," he said and held out his hand.

Harri didn't want to give him her phone but did it anyway. What choice did she have? Her gut told her Debi was here, maybe even Addison. She hoped Tom got her messages. She would be on her own until he did.

She pulled her cell phone out and turned it off before handing it to the security guard. He put a barcode sticker on the back and pulled out a barcode reader to scan a bracelet. He handed the small silver bracelet to her.

"I hope you enjoy yourself, ma'am," he said with a smirk and strolled away.

Harri hadn't realized she was holding her breath until

he was a good twenty feet in the opposite direction of her.

Harri surveyed the grounds to decide where she should search next. Several smaller outbuildings were nestled amongst the thicker grove of trees behind the two bigger buildings. They looked like bungalows, or guest houses to her.

The pool was emptying out as the night grew cooler and couples paired off. The bartenders kept the alcohol flowing freely from small stations dotted around the grounds.

Harri observed that all the men had similar bracelets to the one she had on, but only some women did. The younger looking women, girls really, didn't have them. Did that mean they never turned in their cell phones?

She highly doubted that. What women came to a party without one? These girls were the ones being trafficked, she realized.

Harri swore at herself for not asking Tom for backup immediately. Without her phone though, that ship had sailed. She could only hope he'd come sooner rather than later.

Harri focused back on her search for Debi and Addison, scanning every face she could see for any resemblance to the two missing teenagers. When she'd checked all the faces of the women on the patio, she decided to systematically search every building, going from left to right. She kept her cool demeanor the entire time, making it seem like she was just looking for someone she hadn't yet found yet, which was kind of true.

She calculated she'd been here at least an hour and had gone through three of the bungalows and had two more to search. Choosing the smaller of the two, she walked in and found it had a similar layout to the three before. A kitchen was to the right and a large living space took up the left. A small hallway led back into the darkness between the two rooms. This bungalow looked like it was old as well, with dark paneled wood and intricate details above the small windows. She bet this compound was built in the 1920s or 30s.

Couples spread out everywhere in various stages of undress. No one bothered to look up as she picked her way through the bungalow looking for her two missing girls.

A blonde woman pulled a man into one of the bedrooms, giving Harri only two doors to open. She used the excuse of looking for the bathroom and found one room empty and the other the actual bathroom.

She was running out of places to search. If she didn't find Debi and Addison in the last bungalow where else could she look? In those smaller buildings in the trees? It would be much harder to wander in there looking for a bathroom.

As she stepped out onto the small porch, a flash of copper red hair drew her attention to one of those smaller buildings in the woods. Harri's heart soared in excitement. She'd finally found one of her girls.

35

DAY 4 – EVENING

As soon as Debi felt the cold fresh air on her face, she sucked in as much oxygen as she could. She hadn't had the easiest time walking the distance Bryan Mortimer forced her to. They'd walked past music, chatting people, clinking glasses. The raucous nature of the party made her head spin again, until she got outside, and cold air hit her face.

Everything came into sharp relief then.

She was being held in some sort of colony of bungalows with a pool in the middle. People drank and couples talked around the beautifully lit grounds. She was in the middle of a normal party.

No, that couldn't be right. She'd been living in a tiny room for how many days? Debi wasn't even sure.

One day? All the while being drugged and raped by a famous film director.

She shook her head. This wasn't a dream.

She was outside of her prison in the middle of a party. With people laughing and drinking just outside of her prison cell.

None of this made sense to her. Debi had no clue what day it was or what night it was or how long he'd kept her captive. The drugs had made her lose track of time.

None of that mattered, though.

Debi was out and she was cognizant of everything around her. Not like the other times he'd taken her out of the room. Where those experiences only came in distant, hazy flashes of horror.

Debi stumbled to see how tightly he was holding her. Could she make a run for it now? Scream at all these people to help her.

His strong arms dragged her back up against his body.

"I wish that I could have you tonight," he began. "However, I promised you to some dear friends of mine and I can't go back on my word. A man's word is everything and I never go back on my word."

Debi swallowed down her moan of fear. She wouldn't give him the satisfaction of knowing how terrified she was. She continued to pretend she was more doped up than she was. If she could keep him in the dark about how lucid she was, she'd find a chance to break away.

He brought her around the pool toward two twenty-something looking guys. The two were good-looking enough to maybe be actors and not agents or producers.

They laughed to each other when they saw them, and Debi wondered what they thought was happening. She was barely walking, hardly holding her head up. One arm was around her waist, holding her up while the other held her arm, guiding her. What the hell did they think was happening?

"Bryan, you sure know how to pick them," the brown-haired guy said. He had warm brown eyes and a beautiful smile that showed off a dimple.

Monsters could also appear kind and be good-looking, Debi thought.

Bryan Mortimer was not a bad looking man and with his power and fame and should have been able to get dozens of girls without having to drug them and keep them captive.

The drugs had to be wearing off because her thoughts were more lucid. Debi relaxed her body more, slumping harder against Bryan to appear more out-of-it than she was. Bryan pushed her into the brown-haired guy's arms. He wrapped one arm around her neck and the other around her waist.

"I can't wait to taste of you," he whispered and licked her cheek.

Debi involuntarily whimpered and then inhaled deeply to try to calm the intense fear that was shooting through her body.

"I call sharesies on this one," the second guy said and pulled her body between the two of them.

They touched her like they owned her. One caressed and squeezed her butt while the other one fondled her breasts.

"I've saved you guys a room in bungalow E. It's right behind there," Bryan Mortimer said.

Debi had no idea where 'there' was, as she didn't want to look up. She had to play the drugged-out girl.

Once Bryan left them, she'd make a run for it. She made her body go super slack and leaned into whoever was on her right. She heard him laugh at that and he pinched her hard on her belly.

"I like pliable girls," the guy said.

Debi squeezed her eyes shut and breathed in and out waiting for her chance.

36

DAY 4 – EVENING

Harri stepped out of the bungalow and watched a young woman with copper red hair being dragged towards one of the smaller buildings surrounded by the tall firs. The girl's hair was a similar length and the color was spot on for Debi Mills. The beautiful color glowed in the light from the twinkle lights leading up to the smaller home.

Harri picked her way toward the trio, hoping to stay out of the way of any other partygoers. Most of the party had dispersed inside the many buildings. She was much more out in the open now and without the cover of the crowd.

As she made her way closer to the trio, she caught sight of Bryan Mortimer and stepped behind a tree. She watched him from there as he left Debi with the two guys. He was flanked by two girls who didn't look older than sixteen. They were headed to a smaller bungalow nestled behind some massive cacti.

The man himself was here, she thought.

Debi was here.

Addison had to be here somewhere, too.

She listened for any sounds of sirens but so far all she heard was the thumping of the music.

Once she'd taken care of the two guys, she and Debi would have to storm the gatehouse for her phone. She had her small revolver in her ankle holster, and she'd use it if she had to. Not before getting Debi away from those men.

The brightness of the twinkle lights caused her to stick out as she came closer to the trio. She didn't think the two men who were dragging Debi into the bungalow would notice. She worried more about the security scattered around the party.

She had counted at least twenty security people who were in contact with each other through their earpieces. They were all scattered throughout the grounds, doing a patrol of their sections. Harri wondered when the guard for this section would come back around.

She kept close to the trees and made her way as quietly as she could. The music was still thumping relatively loudly so even if she did crunch on a branch, the sound was hidden by the beat.

A commotion started in front of her and she watched Debi suddenly come to life and try to break away from the two guys. Unfortunately, it was two against one. She managed to shove away from one of them, but the second guy grabbed her around the waist and threw her inside the bungalow.

The door slammed shut.

Harri sprinted the last ten feet and made it onto the small porch without incident. She checked behind her and saw no guards. She put her ear to the door and didn't hear anything from inside. She hoped the layout was like the other buildings she's already searched.

Harri opened the door and slipped inside. To her relief, the layout was the same. Kitchen to the left, small living area to the right with a hallway going toward the back.

Small gasps were coming from the nearest door. Harri guessed that was where the men had Debi.

She around the room. What could she use to hit the men with? She could take on one of them but not two. Harri needed a weapon.

Keeping as silent as possible, she padded over to the kitchenette and looked for a skillet. A skillet was a woman's best weapon. Unless she had a gun, of course. To her disappointment, the kitchenette was only outfitted as a bar with glasses and booze.

Booze.

She grabbed the Jack Daniels bottle by the neck and practiced swinging it around. That would do just fine, she thought.

A scream erupted out of the room.

Harri's pulse quickened. Adrenaline pulsated through her, sharpening her focus. She clutched the bottle tighter.

It was time.

DAY 4 – EVENING

Debi screamed again. The sound didn't stop the guys ripping her clothes off.

One was trying to stick his tongue down her throat while the other one was tearing her dress off her body.

Their hands were everywhere. Terror squeezed her throat.

She desperately bucked trying to get them off her.

They both laughed and she realized it only made them more excited.

Debi tried to lift her knee to attempt a kick. The brown-haired guy easily pinned her leg down with his own.

They were so heavy.

She was losing.

They were going to rape her, and she was awake this time. She'd feel every brutal moment of it. She'd remember every moment of it. The drugs had worn off completely and her body was so weak from lack of food.

She didn't know how long she could keep this up, but she would fight to the bitter end.

Tears ran down Debi's cheeks as she fought hard to wrench her arm away from one of the men.

One of them had his hand up her dress and was pulling off the black lace panties.

This was really happening.

I don't want this. Please. Please somebody help me, her mind screamed.

As if her pleas for help were answered, the door suddenly opened just a bit and a woman snuck into the room holding a liquor bottle.

The woman put a finger to her lips when their eyes met.

The two guys were too busy ravaging her body to notice anything. The brown-haired guy bit her nipple hard and Debi screamed again in pain.

38

DAY 4 – EVENING

Harri put her finger to her lips when she saw Debi's eyes widen. The girl knew she was here to help. She swung the bottle of liquor at the brown-haired guy's head. The bottle connected with a crack. He fell away from Debi, howling in pain.

Harri turned to the second man who charged at her. She punched him in the face with the bottle, breaking his nose.

Blood squirted all over his bare chest.

"What the fuck, bitch," he screamed.

He came at her again trying to head butt her but Harri was too fast. She jumped to the right and when he missed her, she cracked him in the head with the bottle, too. His body thudded to the ground.

She'd knocked him out cold.

The brown-haired guy rose from behind the bed, woozy from the first hit. Harri couldn't take the chance of him alerting anyone else. She smacked him across the head with the bottle again. He went down, hard.

Debi scrambled off the bed and threw herself at Harri.

She dropped the bottle and took the girl in her arms.

"Can you walk?"

"The drugs have worn off, but I haven't eaten in days," Debi said, shaking like a leaf. She was going into shock, Harri thought. She unscrewed the cap off the whiskey.

"Take a sip of this. It'll help," Harri said.

Debi shook her head no and backed away from Harri.

"Debi, it's all right." Harri assured her. "I'm a police detective. I came here to find you."

Debi stared back at Harri. Harri realized Debi thought she might be one of her captors.

"Your roommate Janie sent me." Harri said.

Debi burst into tears.

Harri handed the bottle to Debi who gulped down a large sip and began to cough through her tears.

Harri pulled her out of the room and closed the door behind them.

"We have to get out of here," Debi cried. "He'll come back for me."

"I have to see if anyone else is here," Harri said and pulled her down the hall.

"No, we have to go," Debi begged. "Please. We have to go. They've been keeping me prisoner, we have to get out of here before they see us," Debi wailed.

"Debi, I'm an LAPD detective," Harri explained as calmly as she could. "I'm looking for another girl who's also missing. Have you seen or heard of anyone named Addison? Addison James?"

Debi gulped down a sob and shook her head. She stood in the corner and did her best to pull herself together.

Harri put her ear to the door to see if there was a couple in there. When she didn't hear anything, she tried to open the door. It was locked.

"I'm gonna have to break it down," Harri said. "Stay over there."

Debi obeyed and Harri gave herself enough room to kick the door right next to the doorknob. The door stayed locked.

"I don't think this is going to work," Debi whispered.

Harri closed her eyes and imagined Addison on the other side, held captive for weeks. With a grunt she propelled her shoulder into the door, hitting it as hard as she could. The cheap wood gave way and the door flew open.

Harri groaned with the exploding pain in her shoulder. She'd done it but might have messed up her collarbone again.

"There's a girl in here," cried Debi.

Harri could see she'd found Addison James. The girl lay on a small twin bed, completely passed it out.

"Is she dead?" Debi asked as Harri took her pulse.

"It's okay, Debi." Harri tried to reassure the terrified girl. "I feel a heartbeat. She must be drugged like you were."

"We have to leave her," Debi started crying again. "We won't be able to carry her. Those guys are going to wake up. He'll come back for me."

"We just need to get to the gatehouse. My phone's in there. We'll call the police from there."

"What? What does that mean? You're here by yourself? No one is out there to save us? Oh my god, they're gonna find us and he's gonna put me back in that room," Debi wailed and gasped for air.

Harri put her hands on Debi's shoulders and got close to her face.

"Debi! I know this is hard. I know you're scared. I'm asking a lot of you right now, but you really need to calm down. Nobody's coming for us until I get that damn phone. So, we're going to have to make our way through this entire compound to get there. You can stay here with Addison or you can come with me."

"No," Debi shook her head as she tried to control her tears. "No, please don't leave me here. Those guys are going to wake up."

Harri didn't want to leave Addison behind, but she had no other choice. She grabbed Debi by the hand and pulled her down the hall. The door to the room that Debi had been in was open. The two guys had snuck out.

"We just ran out of time," Harri said.

They ran towards the front door and opened it.

Bryan Mortimer came rushing toward them, his eyes black with fury and his face set to stone.

"No, he has a gun," Debi screamed from behind her.

POP!

POP!

Harri threw herself at Debi and they both tumbled to the ground.

The night erupted with sirens.

Harri pulled Debi out of the doorway and peeked out, fumbling with her ankle holster.

Bryan Mortimer stopped, his face twisting into something ugly and furious. He pointed his gun at Harri. "I'm going get you, bitch," he sneered and then disappeared into the darkness of the woods.

Debi wailed next to her as Harri pulled out her gun and waited.

She could run after him, but she wouldn't give him

the chance to come back and hurt the girls while she was out in the woods getting lost as she searched for him. She would get him. His day would come.

Her shoulder screamed in pain. She positioned herself in the doorway and watched as half-dressed men came stumbling out of the various bungalows.

The red and blue lights of patrol cars illuminated the night. Shouts came from behind the first bungalow and Harri watched the LAPD SWAT team stream in.

She holstered her gun back at her ankle and waited for them to find her.

39

DAY 4 – EVENING

Detective Harri Harper watched as two ambulances drove away carrying Debi Mills and Addison James. Harri had stayed with Debi, LAPD badge in hand, until SWAT found them.

Overall, the bust had netted over eighty arrests and the LAPD had gotten buses to take all the men to booking. The charges were statutory rape so far. Many of the girls without bracelets were under the age of sixteen and had been trafficked to the party.

As Harri watched the paramedics treat Addison, Tom coordinated the search of the entire property. The uniformed officers had found four other girls locked in rooms and heavily drugged.

Harri found Tom near the largest bungalow, watching as CID gathered evidence and the uniformed officers secured the scene.

"How did you get a search warrant this fast?" Harri asked.

"When your text message came in, I mobilized units

and called in a massive favor with a judge I know. He gave me a verbal warrant on the evidence you'd already gathered."

"I worried I didn't give you enough in that text," she said.

"I texted you back almost immediately. When you didn't answer, I had the tech guys ping your phone. When your location sat unchanged, I knew we had to go in."

"You came in the nick of time." Harri smiled at him. "Bryan Mortimer came at us with a gun, You should direct CID to pull any bullets in that bungalow. In case they match with any unsolved cases."

"He ran?"

"He did." Harri sighed. "And a man like that has an escape plan. I'm still unsure how I stumbled on this party. Have we found a woman named Jennifer Randall?"

"I'd have to look on the logs," Tom said. "Lydia Macros gave you our entire case."

"With the girls as witnesses, I think we'll have him," she said. "Even if they fall through, we have him on kidnapping, imprisonment and not to mention the drugs."

"What's going on with your shoulder?" Tom asked. "You need to get checked?"

Harri twisted her back and arm, trying to ease the pain in her shoulder.

"I broke a door down using my body as a ram," she explained. "I'm gonna hurt for a while, but I'll be fine."

One of the uniforms came running toward Tom. "Detective Bards! We found the control room. There are cameras everywhere and TVs and drives," he said, panting between words.

Tom and Harri looked at each other.

"Merry Christmas, Tom." She smiled at him.

"Happy Birthday, Harri." He laughed.

They followed the officer to the first bungalow Harri had searched. The uniform led them through the kitchen and opened what Harri assumed was a cupboard door.

The uniform opened it and Harri peered down at concrete stairs. "I didn't think anyone had basements in LA."

"Wait 'til you see this setup," the officer said as he took the lead down the stairs. "The guys in here scampered away as we were coming. They forgot to lock everything up."

"Lucky for us," Harri said and whistled as a room the size of the entire footprint of the house above appeared. A bank of over thirty video monitors ran alongside one of the walls. A single computer terminal sat in front of the display. The monitors were split into quad frames and showed every corner of the compound, even the bathrooms.

"Perfect setup for some extortion," Harri said to Tom.

She pressed the space bar on the computer terminal with her gloved hand. A screen came up with a single field for a password.

"Damn, it's going to take days for one of our techs to get this thing open," Tom said.

"What about this," Harri said. "Rosebud. Stephen Ladner said that when I interviewed him. Remember how we thought it was a code?"

"We probably have three tries. Rosebud might as well be the first one. Then we can let the techs take over if it doesn't work," Tom said.

"Let's hope we get lucky then," Harri said.

She typed in Rosebud into the password field and the computer turned on and flashed to the home screen.

"We have him," Tom said as Harri opened up the documents tab and found folders with dates. Hundreds of them.

"Thank you, Stephen Ladner," she said.

DAY 5

Harri Harper had her shoulder checked to make sure she hadn't dislocated it again. It was still sore from when she'd hurt herself two months ago up in Oregon and the bruising she gave herself breaking down the door where Addison James was being held hadn't helped the healing process.

She dulled the pain by popping three Extra-Strength Advil. Her lack of sleep wasn't helping her body either.

A massive search was under way for Bryan Mortimer. The crime scene investigators were still working the compound. It would take the teams days before they could collect every bit of evidence. The estate was owned by a shell corporation and Tom had handed that line of inquiry off to the finance crimes investigators.

Digital Techs were combing through the massive amount of videos and images they'd unlocked on the servers in the control room. They'd already found the video of Sophie being assaulted by Bryan Mortimer.

They had him for rape, but not yet for murder. Harri joined Tom in the lobby of Cedars-Sinai Hospital, where

Debi Mills and Addison James had been brought. They'd both received the call that Debi was well enough to talk. She hadn't had as many drugs in her system as Addison did or for as long a time. The doctors were keeping her there for another day for observation.

"Have you slept yet?" Tom asked as they headed toward the elevators.

"Have you?" Harri countered.

Tom laughed. "Ah, the counter question. Classic Harri Harper, no? I directed the retrieval of all the drives from the control room. Call me paranoid. At least, I made sure no drives disappeared and they're safe with our people at cybercrimes."

"I haven't left this waiting room. I don't know why, but it made me feel better to be in the same place as the girls."

"Did you get that shoulder looked at?" he asked.

"Yes. Major bruising, nothing broken. Debi's on the fourth floor," Harri said as they stepped into the elevator.

Tom punched the number four and the elevator doors closed.

"Thank you for saving me," Debi said.

Harri nodded and squeezed her hand. She looked so small in the hospital bed with tubes coming out of her nose and an IV in her arm.

"The doctor said the drugs are almost completely out of your system. You didn't take in as much as they hoped you would?" Harri said.

"It was in the food and water. I started drinking the tap water and not eating. I only pretended. I flushed the bad food down the toilet."

"Smart girl," Tom said in approval.

"I don't really know what day it is, though," Debi said.

"You've been missing three days," Harri said.

Debi was quiet for a moment, taking that in.

"I don't remember much. I was pretty out of it until that last night when I realized what was happening and didn't eat the food or drink the water."

"How did you end up there?" Harri asked.

They'd decided that Harri would do both of the interviews as Tom didn't want to traumatize the girls any further by being interviewed by a man.

"Georgie," Debi said. "It was a woman named Georgie Shipwell. She saw me at one of my auditions and we became friends. She took me to Desmond Ryan's acting class and paid for private lessons."

Debi's tears rolled down her face.

"Debi, none of this was your fault," Harri said.

"I was so stupid though," Debi sobbed. "Here I thought I was some street-smart girl who had managed to keep myself safe for the last two years and I fell for a woman I'd just met promising me the world. She was so nice, though. I mean, she's the daughter of a famous movie star. How could a woman do this to me?"

"It's a betrayal," Harri acknowledged. "You were obviously manipulated. Tell me how she got you to go with her to the party?"

"She wanted to pay for the private lessons with Desmond Ryan and I told her, you know I can't afford that. She said some stuff about giving back and helping struggling artists or something. She seemed for real. Like she really believed in me and my talent." Debi paused to wipe her tears and take a deep breath.

"When I agreed to the lessons, she was happy. Then

she said come meet my friends at this fine Hollywood party. I tried to ask where it was, so I could let Janie know and she said it was a secret because the party was exclusive. I trusted her. When she picked me up in the town car, she gave me champagne to drink and that's the last I remember," Debi said.

"And that's when you woke up in the room?" Harri asked.

"Yes. And I was all messed up. My body hurt and my private parts hurt too," she said and blushed.

"We understand. You had a rape kit done, correct?" she asked.

Debi nodded.

"Do you remember any of the men who did that to you?" Harri asked.

"I woke up that way. I don't remember anyone hurting me until those two men that you knocked out."

"What else can you tell me about Georgie Shipwell? Do you know where she lives? Does she have a regular job that she mentioned?"

"I don't know," Debi said. "She drove a white BMW to Desmond Ryan's. All the casting agents seemed to know her. Like they were friends. She said she had a lot of money and had always had a lot of money. I don't think she liked her dad very much, maybe. I don't know."

"Okay. Just rest now. We can have you come down to the station to make a formal statement for us after you're released," Harri said.

Debi nodded.

Harri and Tom nodded at the uniform guarding Debi's room as the went back out to the hallway.

"She won't be able to testify Bryan Mortimer was the one who took her," Harri said in a low voice. "We need to bring in Georgie Shipwell. I've looked for that name and came up with nothing. Has to be an alias, or maybe a stage name. Debi has her cell number, too."

"That'll be a burner, I'm sure," Tom said, matching Harri's tone. "Addison's awake. I got the text when you were talking with Debi. They're only giving us a couple of minutes with her, though."

"I'm thinking she won't know who took her, either."

"We have him on tape with Sophie Lambert."

"Will that be enough?" Harri asked. "He'll have the best lawyers and so far, he's covered his tracks extremely well."

Harri's stomach was in knots. Could Bryan Mortimer be devious enough to get away with all that he'd done? How would he explain away the captivity? The trafficked girls? And was he the killer who'd taken the lives of those twelve girls Tom had discovered in the old case files? What about Stephen Ladner? His neighbor said she'd heard two male voices besides Stephen's. Was it some of his security team? Was it the two private investigators who'd been following Harri and Tom? And who was behind the wheel of the black sports car that had tried to run Harri off the road? Could it have been Mortimer himself?

"Detective Harper!"

Harri turned at the sound of her name and saw Janie, Debi's roommate, coming down the hall, struggling to carry a huge teddy bear and flower arrangement.

Tom immediately moved forward to take the flower arrangement out of her arms.

"Janie," Harri smiled. "It's nice to see you."

"Likewise," Janie said and then glanced at Debi's room. "How is she?"

Harri wasn't sure what to say. Pretty good, considering?

"I think she'll be over the moon to see you." Harri said.

Tom handed the flower arrangement to the uniformed officer and nodded toward the room. He followed Janie in and closed the door behind him.

Harri and Tom walked down the hall and into Addison James' hospital room. Addison looked like a tiny thing in a large bed and had far more wires than one would think possible sticking out of her.

Mavis James sat next to her bed, holding her daughter's hand.

"You found her for me," she said.

Harri nodded.

"Do you think we could talk to her for a second?" Harri asked.

"Of course."

Mavis James stood and hesitated for a moment until Tom escorted her into the hallway.

Harri sat where Mavis had been and looked down at the girl. Her light brown curls made a halo around her head and she looked perfectly in peace.

Addison opened her eyes and looked at Harri.

"Where's my mom?" she asked.

"She's here," Harri assured her. "She's just right out there in the hallway."

"Hi, my name is Harri. I'm a detective with the LAPD," she said.

"My mom said you're the one who found me," Addison whispered.

"I did," Harri said, choking back a tear. "I found you. Like I promised I would."

"Thank you, Harri."

Harri sat quietly for a moment. She didn't want to interrupt the peacefulness that Addison had found after her horrific ordeal. Then she sighed and did her job.

"Addison, I need to ask you some questions, is that okay?"

Addison nodded in response.

"What happened to you? How did you get into that room?"

"Sophie," Addison said. "My friend Sophie Lambert brought me to this party. I knew we were in trouble the moment we got there. It was some sort of sex party. A producer that Sophie was trying to get a job from invited her and she didn't want to go by herself. Where is Sophie?"

Harri realized no one had told Addison that her best friend was dead. She wasn't well enough yet to handle the news, Harri thought. How could she avoid the topic?

"How did you two get separated?" Harri asked.

"Sophie went looking for the producer and I lost her. I looked for her and found her being led up the stairs by some old guys, so I followed them. I tried to get her away from them and one of them stabbed me with something. I think he injected me with something. I felt a prick on my back, and I remember falling," she said.

"What happened when you woke up?" Harri asked.

Addison turned her face away from Harri and looked for her mom, who was still out in the hallway with Tom.

"It's okay, Addison." Harri reassured her. "None of this was your fault."

"I woke up in a room," Addison said. "I don't know

where I was. I couldn't get out. I was really messed up. I could hardly think. I couldn't' stand."

Harri waited for her to continue.

"I knew someone had sex with me because I hurt down there, and I saw blood on the sheets. And then that's really all that I remember. I would wake up and then blackout again. There was food and sometimes clothes. I never put on the clothes, but then I would wake up wearing them." Addison said.

Harri patted her hand.

"You're doing great, Addison," Harri said. "Did you ever hear the name Georgie Shipwell? Or Bryan Mortimer?" Harri asked.

Addison shook her head no. "Bryan Mortimer? Like the movie director?"

Harri nodded.

"No," Addison shook her head. "No, I don't know. I didn't really see anyone."

"Thank you," Harri said and smiled at Mavis James who was eager to come back into the room. Harri stood up from the chair and left the mother and daughter alone.

"Dammit," Harri said to Tom once she was back in the hallway.

"We have the video. We'll get him on that," Tom said.

Harri nodded.

"I think it's time for you to get some sleep. We have a long road ahead to make our case," he said.

"We have to find him first," Harri said. "He could be on a private jet right now flying to god knows where." Like Jerome Wexler did, Harri thought.

"We'll get him," Tom said. "Good thing about Mortimer is he loved to get his picture taken and he's pretty much a household name. All the looky-loos will be calling us with sightings."

"I hope you're right," Harri said. Exhaustion was hitting her in and she was worried she wouldn't be able to drive home.

Tom nodded at the uniform on Addison's door and walked with her to the elevator.

"Hate to say it, Harri, but you look like shit."

Harri glared at him. "So? You look like shit every day."

"No, I don't. Get some sleep is all I'm saying. You found the girls and they're safe now."

"You're right," Harri sighed. "I'm heading home."

She'd wanted to talk to the girls, and now she had. They had some long hours ahead building the case against Bryan Mortimer. And there was still Stephen Ladner's death and the serial killer Tom had uncovered.

Harri carried those thoughts back to her car. She drove home in the afternoon light, wondering again who'd been following them. Did Bryan Mortimer hire those PI's too? Another thread of the investigation they had to wrap up.

So many threads, she thought as she focused on the road. Last thing she needed to do was get into an accident.

41

DAY 5

Harri Harper dropped her purse on the floor and kicked off her shoes. She heard the door click closed behind her and she reset her alarm. Full body pain streamed through her as she contemplated the stairs to her bedroom.

She groaned and her body screamed in pain as she climbed the first flight. She really was going to have to do something about the stairs. Harri grit her teeth and made it to the second landing. Apparently, the Advil had worn off. She crawled the third set of stairs and heaved herself back on her feet.

She'd made it. Harri dropped face first onto the bed and finally allowed herself to surrender to the deep sleep her body, mind, and soul craved.

Harri's eyes snapped open and she stared into the dark eyes of Bryan Mortimer.

He was on top of her.

On her bed.

In her bedroom and in her house.

He narrowed his eyes at her.

"I told you I'd catch you, bitch," he said with a sneer.

He hadn't had the time to tie her hands before she woke up. He was straddling her at her hips, preventing her from moving. Her arms were free.

In a flash, Harri felt around for her side-table and the heavy wooden lamp on it.

This was going to hurt like hell, she thought. Her fingers felt the wood.

She screamed at the effort of lifting the lamp off the table and crashing it into his head.

He howled in pain and fell off of her.

His body hit the floor with a thump. She turned to see where he'd gone.

That's when she noticed the noose around her neck.

It was a thick white rope, the kind that sailors use for their rigging. She worked her fingers underneath it to pull it looser. Instead, it tightened around her hand and neck.

She turned her head to see Bryan. His head bleeding as he held the end of the rope in the doorway.

The pulley system. Harri realized he must have rigged something in her bedroom while she slept. The noose tightened around her neck. Stars appeared at the fringes of her vision.

He was hoisting her body up. Like he must have done with Stephen.

She felt her upper body leaving the bed. He was stringing her up. Her airway was constricting, and she knew she would lose consciousness soon.

Her mind screamed at her to do something.

She could hardly breathe, even though she still had her hand in between the noose and her neck. She was getting sips of air, but they weren't enough. She was fading into unconsciousness.

Harri knew she had only seconds to react.

It took all her effort to raise her knee and use her other hand to find the ankle holster and her gun.

Thank goodness she had placed it back in her holster. She protected Debi and Addison from him. She'd rescued them. There was no way she was going to let him kill her and get away with all the horror and pain he'd inflicted on so many.

With one finger, she clicked off the switch. The darkness was taking over. She'd run out of breath. The noose was tight, and her hand was making his job go even faster.

Harri had one shot at this.

As she gasped for the little sips of air, she pulled up her hand, her shoulder screaming. She only had one shot.

Do it, she thought as she focused on the blurred image that she thought was Bryan Mortimer's head. Her eyes lost focus.

She pulled the trigger.

Pop.

Pop.

She squeezed off two more rounds.

One of them must have hit because the rope suddenly loosened, and her body fell back to the bed.

She choked and gasped for air, coughing and wheezing.

Harri clawed at the noose. It wasn't loosening.

She used whatever energy she had left to pull her trapped hand away from her neck.

The sips of air became gulps of air.

She breathed in oxygen until the black spots left her

vision. Harri worked the knot on the noose again until the hole was big enough to pull it back over her head. She threw it away from her, sitting upright and gasping.

Where was he? Harri frantically blinked her eyes until her vision came back enough to focus. She must have killed him, because he didn't make a sound.

Then she saw him, slumped against the wall. Her vision cleared and she was again able to focus even though she could barely swallow.

She sat up to get a better view of him. His pants were unzipped, and his hand was still on his exposed penis.

In disgust, Harri realized he must have been masturbating as he was stringing her up. Her bullets had penetrated his chest near his heart. A red bloom of blood marred his white shirt. His features were slack.

She turned away from the gory sight.

She had killed him.

Harri lay back on her bed, catching her breath as her heart thumped wildly in her chest. She started to sob, and then wail, and then she heard someone shrieking in rage and recognized the voice as her own.

42

DAY 12

I t had been a week since Bryan Mortimer had tried to kill Harri in her own home. She had been cleared of his death several days later.

It was an open and shut self-defense situation, seeing as he'd broken into her home and strung her up to kill her in her own bedroom.

Detective Tom Bards and his teams found evidence in Mortimer's compound of the drugs he'd used on the girls. They also found a treasure trove of trophies he'd kept from over eighteen girls that had gone missing or died in the last twenty years. Tom found Stephen Ladner's research and article among his trophies. He'd killed Ladner too and tried to make it look like suicide

Bryan Mortimer had kept a library of videos and photos of the girls he'd killed and the hundreds of girls he'd kidnapped, drugged, raped, and trafficked.

Harri couldn't believe the stupidity of keeping all that evidence, but that's how narcissists were. He wanted his own archive of all the things he'd done. It all came down to how invincible he'd felt. He never believed he'd get caught.

At least four famous actresses were part of the evidence gathered at his home, and Tom Bards had taken pains to keep their names out of the media.

The ensuing media circus Tom had anticipated had almost overtaken the case.

A cop had shot one of the most famous directors in the world in her own home as he tried to string her up in a noose. The story grew more sensational by the hour as the news broke of Bryan Mortimer's numerous victims. He'd been both a serial killer and a serial rapist who'd tortured and kept captive so many aspiring young actresses.

Lieutenant Richard Byrne was all over the case and as Tom gathered the evidence to implicate his co-conspirators, like Georgie Shipwell and the men who had been caught up in the sweep at the party, Byrne was busy putting his face in front of every reporter's camera that he could.

It was a massive case, almost bigger than the Creek Killer case because of who Bryan Mortimer was. The case fed the public's appetite for sensationalism. It had everything the media needed to keep the story churning out. Sex. Money. Fame. Hollywood. Glamour. Drugs. Beautiful Innocent Girls.

Harri had been in the hospital for two days after her ordeal and she was now on leave. She was only too happy to hand the case over to Tom Bards and RHD to deal with.

In the meantime, Jake had found a connection between Jerome Wexler and Bryan Mortimer. His FBI contacts had also found evidence of his possible whereabouts in Berlin.

Jake wouldn't leave her side while she was in the hospital. His guilt and rage at not being with her when Mortimer broke into her home, was easy to see, but Harry wished he could let it go. She knew why he couldn't, but she wished she could help him find a way to let his rage go. Maybe, she hoped, if she could find a way to help Jake, she could help herself let go of her own rage, too.

But first she had to recuperate. She'd been in the hospital for two days with bruising around her throat and internal lacerations of her trachea. Her voice box was still traumatized, and her voice came out in a scratchy whisper.

"How's my patient doing?" Jake Tepesky asked as he brought in a tray of breakfast for her.

He'd done an amazing job of cheering her up and soothing her psyche. She had nightmares of waking up with the noose around her neck but couldn't scream. Another nightmare to add to her long list of fears in the middle of the night.

"So, how's my darling patient this morning?" Jake asked as he put her breakfast of oatmeal and warm milk on her lap.

Harri nodded her head and smiled. Jake scolded her for talking unless it was necessary.

"You're being released today, the doctor just told me," Jake said. "So, we need to decide about your going home."

"No stairs," she croaked.

Jake smiled. "Well, about that." What do you think about moving in together?"

Harri looked up at him in surprise and then couldn't help but smile and nod.

Jake's smile matched hers. "I was hoping you'd say

that." He sat down at the edge of her bed and took her hand in his.

"Harri, you can't go back to your house. I hired some crime scene cleaners to…take care of things, but I don't think you can go back there."

Harri was quiet for a moment, and then she nodded in agreement.

"This is what I'm thinking, and I want to know how you feel. We both need a fresh start. And you hate climbing the stairs to my house, even though I have incredible views. So, what if we get a new place? Someplace that's not Harri, not Jake, but that's both of us. A place that's just ours. What do you say?"

Jake watched her as she struggled to hold back her tears.

Finally, she nodded and whispered, "no stairs."

Jake laughed and kissed her. "No stairs," he said. "I promise."

Their flight to Berlin was scheduled for the next week, and she needed to focus on getting her voice back. The doctor had told her that if she didn't speak and was careful not to move her neck, then she might be able to recover enough to get on a plane then.

That's exactly what she was going to do.

ABOUT DOMINIKA BEST

Dominika Best is the author of the Harriet Harper Thriller Series and the Los Angeles Ghosts series.

For more information:
www.dominikabest.com
hello@dominikabest.com

Made in United States
Troutdale, OR
09/19/2023

13027547R00183